Glinda of OZ

by L. Frank Baum

Illustrations by John R. Neill

Another story about the Land of Oz
by the author of

THE WIZARD OF OZ

THE MARVELLOUS LAND OF OZ

Also available in Armada

*This Book is Dedicated to my Son
Robert Stanton Baum*

First published in the U.S.A. about 1920
First published in the U.K. in 1974 by
William Collins Sons & Co. Ltd.,
14 St. James's Place, London, s.w.1

Printed in Great Britain by
Richard Clay (The Chaucer Press), Ltd.,
Bungay, Suffolk

Contents

I

The Call of Duty

GLINDA, the good Sorceress of Oz, sat in the grand court of her palace, surrounded by her maids of honour – a hundred of the most beautiful girls of the Fairyland of Oz. The palace court was built of rare marbles, exquisitely polished. Fountains tinkled musically here and there; the vast colonnade, open to the south, allowed the maidens, as they raised their heads from their embroideries, to gaze upon a vista of rose-hued fields and groves of trees bearing fruits or laden with sweet-scented flowers. At times one of the girls would start a song, the others joining in the chorus, or one would rise and dance, gracefully swaying to the music of a harp played by a companion. And then Glinda smiled, glad to see her maids mixing play with work.

Presently among the fields an object was seen moving, threading the broad path that led to the castle gate. Some of the girls looked upon this object enviously; the Sorceress merely gave it a glance and nodded her stately head as if pleased, for it meant the coming of her friend and mistress – the only one in all the land that Glinda bowed to.

Then up the path trotted a wooden animal attached to a red wagon, and as the quaint steed halted at the gate there descended from the wagon two young girls, Ozma, Ruler of Oz, and her companion, Princess Dorothy. Both were dressed in simple white muslin gowns, and as they ran up the marble steps of the palace they laughed and chatted as gaily as if they were not the most important persons in the world's loveliest fairyland.

The maids of honour had risen and stood with bowed heads to greet the royal Ozma, while Glinda came forward with outstretched arms to greet her guests.

'We've just come on a visit, you know,' said Ozma. 'Both Dorothy and I were wondering how we should pass the day when we happened to think we'd not been to your Quodling Country for weeks, so we took the Sawhorse and rode straight here.'

'And we came so fast,' added Dorothy, 'that our hair is blown all fuzzy, for the Sawhorse makes a wind of his own. Usually it's a day's journey from the Em'rald City, but I don't s'pose we were two hours on the way.'

'You are most welcome,' said Glinda the Sorceress, and led them through the court to her magnificent reception hall. Ozma took the arm of her hostess, but Dorothy lagged behind, kissing some of the maids she knew best, talking with others, and making them all feel that she was their friend. When at last she joined Glinda and Ozma in the reception hall, she found them talking earnestly about the condition of the people, and how to make them more happy and contented – although they were already the happiest and most contented folks in all the world.

This interested Ozma, of course, but it didn't interest Dorothy very much, so the little girl ran over to a big table on which was lying open Glinda's Great Book of Records.

This Book is one of the greatest treasures in Oz, and the Sorceress prizes it more highly than any of her magical possessions. That is the reason it is firmly attached to the big marble table by means of golden chains, and whenever Glinda leaves home she locks the Great Book together with five jewelled padlocks and carries the keys safely hidden in her bosom.

I do not suppose there is any magical thing in any fairy-land to compare with the Record Book, on the pages of which are constantly being printed a record of every event that happens in any part of the world, at exactly the moment it happens. And the records are always truthful, although sometimes they do not give as many details as one could wish. But then, lots of things happen, and so the records have to be brief or even Glinda's Great Book could not hold them all.

Glinda looked at the records several times each day, and Dorothy, whenever she visited the Sorceress, loved to look in the Book and see what was happening everywhere. Not much was recorded about the Land of Oz, which is usually peaceful and uneventful, but today Dorothy found something which interested her. Indeed, the printed letters were appearing on the page even while she looked.

'This is funny!' she exclaimed. 'Did you know, Ozma, that there were people in your Land of Oz called Skeezers?'

'Yes,' replied Ozma, coming to her side, 'I know that on Professor Wogglebug's Map of the Land of Oz there is a place marked "Skeezer", but what the Skeezers are like I do not know. No one I know has ever seen them or heard of them. The Skeezer Country is 'way at the upper edge of the Gillikin Country, with the sandy, impassable desert on one side and the mountains of Oogaboo on another side. That is a part of the Land of Oz of which I know very little.'

'I guess no one else knows much about it either, unless it's the Skeezers themselves,' remarked Dorothy. 'But the Book says: "The Skeezers of Oz have declared war on the Flatheads of Oz, and there is likely to be fighting and much trouble as the result." '

'Is that all the Book says?' asked Ozma.

'Every word,' said Dorothy, and Ozma and Glinda both looked at the Record and seemed surprised and perplexed.

'Tell me, Glinda,' said Ozma, 'who are the Flatheads?'

'I cannot, your Majesty,' confessed the Sorceress. 'Until

now I never have heard of them, nor have I ever heard the
Skeezers mentioned. In the far away corners of Oz are
hidden many curious tribes of people, and those who never
leave their own countries and never are visited by those
from our favoured part of Oz, naturally are unknown to me.
However, if you so desire, I can learn through my arts of
sorcery something of the Skeezers and the Flatheads.'

'I wish you would,' answered Ozma seriously. 'You see,
Glinda, if these are Oz people they are my subjects, and I
cannot allow any wars or troubles in the Land I rule, if I
can possibly help it.'

'Very well, your Majesty,' said the Sorceress, 'I will try
to get some information to guide you. Please excuse me for
a time, while I retire to my Room of Magic and Sorcery.'

'May I go with you?' asked Dorothy, eagerly.

'No, Princess,' was the reply. 'It would spoil the charm
to have anyone present.'

So Glinda locked herself in her own Room of Magic and
Dorothy and Ozma waited patiently for her to come out
again.

In about an hour Glinda appeared, looking grave and
thoughtful.

'Your Majesty,' she said to Ozma, 'the Skeezers live on a
Magic Isle in a great lake. For that reason – because the
Skeezers deal in magic – I can learn little about them.'

'Why, I didn't know there was a lake in that part of Oz,'
exclaimed Ozma. 'The map shows a river running through
the Skeezer Country, but no lake.'

'That is because the person who made the map never
had visited that part of the country,' explained the Sorceress.
'The lake surely is there, and in the lake is an island – a
Magic Isle – and on that island live the people called the
Skeezers.'

'What are they like?' inquired the Ruler of Oz.

'My magic cannot tell me that,' confessed Glinda, 'for the magic of the Skeezers prevents anyone outside of their domain knowing anything about them.'

'The Flatheads must know, if they're going to fight the Skeezers,' suggested Dorothy.

'Perhaps so,' Glinda replied, 'but I can get little information concerning the Flatheads either. They are people who inhabit a mountain just south of the Lake of the Skeezers. The mountain has steep sides and a broad, hollow top, like a basin, and in this basin the Flatheads have their dwellings. They also are magic-workers and usually keep to themselves and allow no one from outside to visit them. I have learned that the Flatheads number about one hundred people – men, women and children – while the Skeezers number just one hundred and one.'

'What did they quarrel about, and why do they wish to fight one another?' was Ozma's next question.

'I cannot tell your Majesty that,' said Glinda.

'But see here!' cried Dorothy, 'it's against the law for anyone but Glinda and the Wizard to work magic in the Land of Oz, so if these two strange people are magic-makers they are breaking the law and ought to be punished!'

Ozma smiled upon her little friend.

'Those who do not know me or my laws,' she said, 'cannot be expected to obey my laws. If we know nothing of the Skeezers or the Flatheads, it is likely that they know nothing of us.'

'But they *ought* to know, Ozma, and we ought to know. Who's going to tell them, and how are we going to make them behave?'

'That,' returned Ozma, 'is what I am now considering. What would you advise, Glinda?'

The Sorceress took a little time to consider this question, before she made reply. Then she said:

'Had you not learned of the existence of the Flatheads and the Skeezers, through my Book of Records, you would never have worried about them or their quarrels. So, if you pay no attention to these peoples, you may never hear of them again.'

'But that wouldn't be right,' declared Ozma. 'I Am Ruler of all the Land of Oz, which includes the Gillikin Country, the Quadling Country, the Winkie Country and the Munchkin Country, as well as the Emerald City, and being the Princess of this fairyland it is my duty to make all my people – wherever they may be – happy and content and to settle their disputes and keep them from quarrelling. So, while the Skeezers and Flatheads may not know me or that I am their lawful Ruler, I now know that they inhabit my kingdom and are my subjects, so I would not be doing my duty if I kept away from them and allowed them to fight.'

'That's a fact, Ozma,' commented Dorothy. 'You've got to go up to the Gillikin Country and make these people behave themselves and make up their quarrels. But how are you going to do it?'

'That is what is puzzling me also, your Majesty,' said the Sorceress. 'It may be dangerous for you to go into those strange countries, where the people are possibly fierce and warlike.'

'I am not afraid,' said Ozma, with a smile.

''Tisn't a question of being 'fraid,' argued Dorothy. 'Of course we know you're a fairy, and can't be killed or hurt, and we know you've a lot of magic of your own to help you. But, Ozma dear, in spite of all this you've been in trouble before, on account of wicked enemies, and it isn't right for the Ruler of all Oz to put herself in danger.'

'Perhaps I shall be in no danger at all,' returned Ozma, with a little laugh. 'You mustn't *imagine* danger, Dorothy, for one should only imagine nice things, and we do not know that the Skeezers and Flatheads are wicked people or my enemies. Perhaps they would be good and listen to reason.'

'Dorothy is right, your Majesty,' asserted the Sorceress. 'It is true we know nothing of these far-away subjects, except that they intend to fight one another, and have a certain amount of magic power at their command. Such folks do not like to submit to interference and they are more likely to resent your coming among them than to receive you kindly and graciously, as is your due.'

. 'If you had an army to take with you,' added Dorothy, 'it wouldn't be so bad; but there isn't such a thing as an army in all Oz.'

'I have one soldier,' said Ozma.

'Yes, the soldier with the green whiskers; but he's dreadful 'fraid of his gun and never loads it. I'm sure he'd run rather than fight. And one soldier, even if he were brave, couldn't do much against two hundred and one Flatheads and Skeezers.'

'What then, my friends, would you suggest?' inquired Ozma.

'I advise you to send the Wizard of Oz to them, and let him inform them that it is against the laws of Oz to fight, and that you command them to settle their differences and become friends,' proposed Glinda. 'Let the Wizard tell them they will be punished if they refuse to obey the commands of the Princess of all the Land of Oz.'

Ozma shook her head, to indicate that the advice was not to her satisfaction.

'If they refuse, what then?' she asked. 'I should be obliged to carry out my threat and punish them, and that would be an unpleasant and difficult thing to do. I am sure it would be better for me to go peacefully, without an army and armed only with my authority as Ruler, and plead with them to obey me. Then, if they prove obstinate I could resort to other means to win their obedience.'

'It's a ticklish thing, anyhow you look at it,' sighed Dorothy. 'I'm sorry now that I noticed the Record in the Great Book.'

'But can't you realize, my dear, that I must do my duty, now that I am aware of this trouble?' asked Ozma. 'I am fully determined to go at once to the Magic Isle of the Skeezers and to the enchanted mountain of the Flatheads, and prevent war and strife between their inhabitants. The only question to decide is whether it is better for me to go alone, or to assemble a party of my friends and loyal supporters to accompany me.'

'If you go I want to go, too,' declared Dorothy. 'Whatever happens it's going to be fun – 'cause all excitement is fun – and I wouldn't miss it for the world!'

Neither Ozma nor Glinda paid any attention to this statement, for they were gravely considering the serious aspect of this proposed adventure.

'There are plenty of friends who would like to go with you,' said the Sorceress; 'but none of them would afford your Majesty any protection in case you were in danger. You are yourself the most powerful fairy in Oz, although both I and the Wizard have more varied arts of magic at our command. However, you have one art that no other in all the world can equal – the art of winning hearts and making people love to bow to your gracious presence. For that reason I believe you can accomplish more good alone than with a large number of subjects in your train.'

'I believe that also,' agreed the Princess. 'I shall be quite able to take care of myself, you know, but might not be able to protect others so well. I do not look for opposition, however, I shall speak to these people in kindly words and settle their dispute – whatever it may be – in a just manner.'

'Aren't you going to take *me*?' pleaded Dorothy. 'You'll need *some* companion, Ozma.'

The Princess smiled upon her little friend.

'I see no reason why you should not accompany me,' was her reply. 'Two girls are not very warlike and they will not suspect us of being on any errand but a kindly and peaceful one. But, in order to prevent war and strife between these angry peoples, we must go to them at once. Let us return immediately to the Emerald City and prepare to start on our journey early tomorrow morning.'

Glinda was not quite satisfied with this plan, but could not think of any better way to meet the problem. She knew that Ozma, with all her gentleness and sweet disposition, was accustomed to abide by any decision she had made and could not easily be turned from her purpose. Moreover she could see no great danger to the fairy Ruler of Oz in the undertaking, even though the unknown people she was to visit proved obstinate. But Dorothy was not a fairy; she was a little girl who had come from Kansas to live in the Land of Oz. Dorothy might encounter dangers that to Ozma would be as nothing but to an 'Earth child' would be very serious.

The very fact that Dorothy lived in Oz, and had been made a Princess by her friend Ozma, prevented her from being killed or suffering any great bodily pain as long as she lived in that fairyland. She could not grow big, either, and would always remain the same little girl who had come to Oz, unless in some way she left that fairyland or was spirited away from it. But Dorothy was a mortal, nevertheless, and might possibly be destroyed, or hidden where none of her friends could ever find her. She could, for instance, be cut into pieces, and the pieces, while still alive and free from pain, could be widely scattered; or she might be buried deep underground, or 'destroyed' in other ways by evil magicians, were she not properly protected. These facts Glinda was considering while she paced with stately tread her marble hall.

Finally the good Sorceress paused and drew a ring from her finger, handing it to Dorothy.

'Wear this ring constantly until you return,' she said to the girl. 'If serious danger threatens you, turn the ring around on your finger once to the right and another turn to the left. That will ring the alarm bell in my palace and I will at once come to your rescue. But do not use the ring unless you are actually in danger of destruction. While you remain with Princess Ozma I believe she will be able to protect you from all lesser ills.'

'Thank you, Glinda,' responded Dorothy gratefully, as she placed the ring on her finger. 'I'm going to wear my Magic Belt which I took from the Gnome King, too, so I guess I'll be safe from anything the Skeezers and Flatheads try to do to me.'

Ozma had many arrangements to make before she could leave her throne and her palace in the Emerald City, even for a trip of a few days, so she bade good-bye to Glinda and with Dorothy climbed into the Red Wagon. A word to the wooden Sawhorse started that astonishing creature on the return journey, and so swiftly did they run that Dorothy was unable to talk or do anything but hold tight to her seat all the way back to the Emerald City.

2

Ozma and Dorothy

RESIDING in Ozma's palace at this time was a live Scarecrow, a most remarkable and intelligent creature who had once ruled the Land of Oz for a brief period and was much loved and respected by all the people. Once a Munchkin farmer had stuffed an old suit of clothes with straw and put stuffed boots on the feet and used a pair of stuffed cotton gloves for hands. The head of the Scarecrow was a stuffed sack fastened to the body, with eyes, nose, mouth and ears painted on the sack. When a hat had been put on the head, the thing was a good imitation of a man. The farmer placed the Scarecrow on a pole in his cornfield and it came to life in a curious manner. Dorothy, who was passing by the field, was hailed by the live Scarecrow and lifted him off his pole. He then went with her to the Emerald City, where the Wizard of Oz gave him some excellent brains, and the Scarecrow soon became an important personage.

Ozma considered the Scarecrow one of her best friends and most loyal subjects, so the morning after her visit to Glinda she asked him to take her place as Ruler of the Land of Oz while she was absent on a journey, and the Scarecrow at once consented without asking any questions.

Ozma had warned Dorothy to keep their journey a secret and say nothing to anyone about the Skeezers and Flatheads until their return, and Dorothy promised to obey. She longed to tell her girl friends, tiny Trot and Betsy Bobbin, of the adventure they were undertaking, but refrained from saying a word on the subject although both these girls lived with her in Ozma's palace.

Indeed, only Glinda the Sorceress knew they were going, until after they had gone, and even the Sorceress didn't know what their errand might be.

Princess Ozma took the Sawhorse and the Red Wagon, although she was not sure there was a wagon road all the way to the Lake of the Skeezers. The Land of Oz is a pretty big place, surrounded on all sides by a Deadly Desert which it is impossible to cross, and the Skeezer Country, according to the map, was in the farthest north-western part of Oz, bordering on the north desert. As the Emerald City was exactly in the centre of Oz, it was no small journey from there to the Skeezers.

Around the Emerald City the country is thickly settled in every direction, but the farther away you get from the city the fewer people there are, until those parts that border on the desert have small populations. Also those far-away sections are little known to the Oz people, except in the south, where Glinda lives and where Dorothy has often wandered on trips of exploration.

The least known of all is the Gillikin Country, which harbours many strange bands of people among its mountains and valleys and forests and streams, and Ozma was now bound for the most distant part of the Gillikin Country.

'I am really sorry,' said Ozma to Dorothy, as they rode away in the Red Wagon, 'not to know more about the wonderful Land I rule. It is my duty to be acquainted with every tribe of people and every strange and hidden country in all Oz, but I am kept so busy at my palace making laws and planning for the comforts of those who live near the Emerald City, that I do not often find time to make long journeys.'

'Well,' replied Dorothy, 'we'll prob'bly find out a lot on this trip, and we'll learn all about the Skeezers and Flatheads, anyhow. Time doesn't make much diff'rence in the

Land of Oz, 'cause we don't grow up, or get old, or become sick and die, as they do other places; so, if we explore one place at a time, we'll by-an'-by know all about every nook and corner in Oz.'

Dorothy wore around her waist the Gnome King's Magic Belt, which protected her from harm, and the Magic Ring which Glinda had given her was on her finger. Ozma had merely slipped a small silver wand into the bosom of her gown, for fairies do not use chemicals and herbs and the tools of wizards and sorcerers to perform their magic. The Silver Wand was Ozma's one weapon of offence and defence and by its use she could accomplish many things.

They had left the Emerald City just at sunrise and the Sawhorse travelled very swiftly over the roads toward the north, but in a few hours the wooden animal had to slacken his pace because the farm houses had become few and far between and often there were no paths at all in the direction they wished to follow. At such times they crossed the fields, avoiding groups of trees and fording the streams and rivulets whenever they came to them. But finally they reached a broad hillside closely covered with scrubby brush, through which the wagon could not pass.

'It will be difficult even for you and me to get through without tearing our dresses,' said Ozma, 'so we must leave the Sawhorse and the Wagon here until our return.'

'That's all right,' Dorothy replied, 'I'm tired riding, anyhow. Do you s'pose, Ozma, we're anywhere near the Skeezer Country?'

'I cannot tell, Dorothy dear, but I know we've been going in the right direction, so we are sure to find it in time.'

The scrubby brush was almost like a grove of small trees, for it reached as high as the heads of the two girls, neither of whom was very tall. They were obliged to thread their way in and out, until Dorothy was afraid they would get lost, and finally they were halted by a curious thing that barred their farther progress. It was a huge web – as if woven by gigantic spiders – and the delicate, lacy film was fastened stoutly to the branches of the bushes and continued to the right and left in the form of a half circle. The threads of this web were of a brilliant purple colour and woven into numerous artistic patterns, but it reached from the ground to branches above the heads of the girls and formed a sort of fence that hedged them in.

'It doesn't look very strong, though,' said Dorothy. 'I wonder if we couldn't break through.' She tried but found the web stronger than it seemed. All her efforts could not break a single thread.

'We must go back, I think, and try to get around this peculiar web,' Ozma decided.

So they turned to the right and, following the web, found that it seemed to spread in a regular circle. On and on they went until finally Ozma said they had returned to the exact spot from which they had started. 'Here is a handkerchief you dropped when we were here before,' she said to Dorothy.

'In that case, they must have built the web behind us, after we walked into the trap,' exclaimed the little girl.

'True,' agreed Ozma, 'an enemy has tried to imprison us.'

'And they did it, too,' said Dorothy. 'I wonder who it was.'

'It's a spider-web, I'm quite sure,' returned Ozma, 'but it must be the work of enormous spiders.'

'Quite right!' cried a voice behind them. Turning quickly around they beheld a huge purple spider sitting not two yards away and regarding them with its small bright eyes.

Then there crawled from the bushes a dozen more great purple spiders, which saluted the first one and said:

'The web is finished, O King, and the strangers are our prisoners.'

Dorothy did not like the looks of these spiders at all. They had big heads, sharp claws, small eyes and fuzzy hair all over their purple bodies.

'They look wicked,' she whispered to Ozma. 'What shall we do?'

Ozma gazed upon the spiders with a serious face.

'What is your object in making us prisoners?' she inquired.

'We need someone to keep house for us,' answered the Spider King. 'There is sweeping and dusting to be done, and polishing and washing of dishes, and that is work my people dislike to do. So we decided that if any strangers came our way we would capture them and make them our servants.'

'I am Princess Ozma, Ruler of all Oz,' said the girl with dignity.

'Well, I am King of all Spiders,' was the reply, 'and that makes me your master. Come with me to my palace and I will instruct you in your work.'

'I won't,' said Dorothy indignantly. 'We won't have anything to do with you.'

'We'll see about that,' returned the Spider in a severe tone, and the next instant he made a dive straight at Dorothy, opening the claws on his legs as if to grab and pinch her with the sharp points. But the girl was wearing her Magic Belt and was not harmed. The Spider King could not even touch her.

He turned swiftly and made a dash at Ozma, but she held her Magic Wand over his head and the monster recoiled as if it had been struck.

'You'd better let us go,' Dorothy advised him, 'for you see you can't hurt us.'

'So I see,' returned the Spider King angrily. 'Your magic is greater than mine. But I'll not help you to escape. If you can break the magic web my people have woven you may go; if not you must stay here and starve.' With that the Spider King uttered a peculiar whistle and all the spiders disappeared.

'There is more magic in my fairyland than I dreamed of,' remarked the beautiful Ozma, with a sigh of regret. 'It seems that my laws have not been obeyed, for even these monstrous spiders defy me by means of magic.'

'Never mind that now,' said Dorothy; 'let's see what we can do to get out of this trap.'

They now examined the web with great care and were amazed at its strength. Although finer than the finest silken hairs, it resisted all their efforts to work through, even though both girls threw all their weight against it.

'We must find some instrument which will cut the threads

of the web,' said Ozma, finally. 'Let us look about for such a tool.'

So they wandered among the bushes and finally came to a shallow pool of water, formed by a small bubbling spring. Dorothy stooped to get a drink and discovered in the water a green crab, about as big as her hand. The crab had two big, sharp claws, and as soon as Dorothy saw them she had an idea that those claws could save them.

'Come out of the water,' she called to the crab; 'I want to talk to you.'

Rather lazily the crab rose to the surface and caught hold of a bit of rock. With his head above the water he said in a cross voice:

'What do you want?'

'We want you to cut the web of the purple spiders with your claws, so we can get through it,' answered Dorothy. 'You can do that, can't you?'

'I suppose so,' replied the crab. 'But if I do what will you give me?'

'What do you wish?' Ozma inquired.

'I wish to be white, instead of green,' said the crab. 'Green crabs are very common, and white ones are rare; besides the purple spiders, which infest this hillside, are afraid of white crabs. Could you make me white if I should agree to cut the web for you?'

'Yes,' said Ozma, 'I can do that easily. And so you may know I am speaking the truth, I will change your colour now.'

She waved her silver wand over the pool and the crab instantly became snow-white – all except his eyes, which remained black. The creature saw his reflection in the water and was so delighted that he at once climbed out of the pool and began moving slowly toward the web, by backing away from the pool. He moved so very slowly that Dorothy cried out impatiently: 'Dear me, this will never do!' Catching the crab in her hands she ran with him to the web.

She had to hold him up even then, so he could reach with his claws strand after strand of the filmy purple web, which he was able to sever with one nip.

When enough of the web had been cut to allow them to pass, Dorothy ran back to the pool and placed the white crab in the water, after which she rejoined Ozma. They were just in time to escape through the web, for several of the purple spiders now appeared, having discovered that their web had been cut, and had the girls not rushed through the opening the spiders would have quickly repaired the cuts and again imprisoned them.

Ozma and Dorothy ran as fast as they could and although the angry spiders threw a number of strands of web after them, hoping to lasso them or entangle them in the coils, they managed to escape and clamber to the top of the hill.

3

The Mist Maidens

FROM the top of the hill Ozma and Dorothy looked down into the valley beyond and were surprised to find it filled with a floating mist that was as dense as smoke. Nothing in the valley was visible except these rolling waves of mist, but beyond, on the other side, rose a grassy hill that appeared quite beautiful.

'Well,' said Dorothy, 'what are we to do, Ozma? Walk down into that thick fog, an' prob'bly get lost in it, or wait till it clears away?'

'I'm not sure it will clear away, however long we wait,' replied Ozma, doubtfully. 'If we wish to get on, I think we must venture into the mist.'

'But we can't see where we're going, or what we're stepping on,' protested Dorothy. 'There may be dreadful things mixed up in that fog, an' I'm scared just to think of wading into it.'

Even Ozma seemed to hesitate. She was silent and thoughtful for a little while, looking at the rolling drifts that were so grey and forbidding. Finally she said:

'I believe this is a Mist Valley, where these moist clouds always remain, for even the sunshine above does not drive them away. Therefore the Mist Maids must live here, and they are fairies and should answer my call.'

She placed her two hands before her mouth, forming a hollow with them, and uttered a clear, trilling, bird-like cry. It floated far out over the mist waves and presently was answered by a similar sound, as of a far-off echo.

Dorothy was much impressed. She had seen many strange things since coming to this fairy country, but here was a new experience. At ordinary times Ozma was just like any little girl one might chance to meet – simple, merry, lovable as could be – yet with a certain reserve that lent her dignity in her most joyous moods. There were times, however, when seated on her throne and commanding her subjects, or when her fairy powers were called into use, when Dorothy and all others about her stood in awe of their lovely girl Ruler and realized her superiority.

Ozma waited. Presently out from the billows rose beautiful forms, clothed in fleecy, trailing garments of grey that could scarcely be distinguished from the mist. Their hair was mist-colour, too; only their gleaming arms and sweet, pallid faces proved they were living, intelligent creatures answering the call of a sister fairy.

Like sea nymphs they rested on the bosom of the clouds, their eyes turned questioningly upon the two girls who stood upon the bank. One came quite near and to her Ozma said:

'Will you please take us to the opposite hillside? We are afraid to venture into the mist. I am Princess Ozma of Oz, and this is my friend Dorothy, a Princess of Oz.'

The Mist Maids came nearer, holding out their arms. Without hesitation Ozma advanced and allowed them to embrace her and Dorothy plucked up courage to follow. Very gently the Mist Maids held them. Dorothy thought the arms were cold and misty – they didn't seem real at all – yet they supported the two girls above the surface of the billows and floated with them so swiftly to the green hillside opposite that the girls were astonished to find themselves set upon the grass before they realized they had fairly started.

'Thank you!' said Ozma gratefully, and Dorothy also added her thanks for the service.

The Mist Maids made no answer, but they smiled and waved their hands in good-bye as again they floated out into the mist and disappeared from view.

4

The Magic Tent

'WELL,' said Dorothy with a laugh, 'that was easier than I expected. It's worth while, sometimes, to be a real fairy. But I wouldn't like to be that kind, and live in a dreadful fog all the time.'

They now climbed the bank and found before them a delightful plain that spread for miles in all directions. Fragrant wild flowers were scattered throughout the grass; there were bushes bearing lovely blossoms and luscious fruits; now and then a group of stately trees added to the beauty of the landscape. But there were no dwellings or signs of life.

The farther side of the plain was bordered by a row of palms, and just in front of the palms rose a queerly shaped hill that towered above the plain like a mountain. The sides of this hill were straight up and down; it was oblong in shape and the top seemed flat and level.

'Oh, ho!' cried Dorothy; 'I'll bet that's the mountain Glinda told us of, where the Flatheads live.'

'If it is,' replied Ozma, 'the Lake of the Skeezers must be just beyond the line of palm trees. Can you walk that far, Dorothy?'

'Of course, in time,' was the prompt answer. 'I'm sorry we had to leave the Sawhorse and the Red Wagon behind us, for they'd come in handy just now; but with the end of our journey in sight a tramp across these pretty green fields won't tire us a bit.'

It was a longer tramp than they suspected, however, and

night overtook them before they could reach the flat mountain. So Ozma proposed they camp for the night and Dorothy was quite ready to approve. She didn't like to admit to her friend she was tired, but she told herself that her legs 'had prickers in 'em', meaning they had begun to ache.

Usually when Dorothy started on a journey of exploration or adventure, she carried with her a basket of food, and other things that a traveller in a strange country might require, but to go away with Ozma was quite a different thing, as experience had taught her. The fairy Ruler of Oz only needed her silver wand – tipped at one end with a great sparkling emerald – to provide through its magic all that they might need. Therefore Ozma, having halted with her companion and selected a smooth, grassy spot on the plain, waved her wand in graceful curves and chanted some mystic words in her sweet voice, and in an instant a handsome tent appeared before them. The canvas was striped purple and white, and from the centre pole fluttered the royal banner of Oz.

'Come, dear,' said Ozma, taking Dorothy's hand, 'I am hungry and I'm sure you must be also; so let us go in and have our feast.'

On entering the tent they found a table set for two, with snowy linen, bright silver and sparkling glassware, a vase of roses in the centre and many dishes of delicious food, some smoking hot, waiting to satisfy their hunger. Also, on either side of the tent were beds, with satin sheets, warm blankets and pillows filled with swansdown. There were chairs, too, and tall lamps that lighted the interior of the tent with a soft, rosy glow.

Dorothy, resting herself at her fairy friend's command, and eating her dinner with unusual enjoyment, thought of the wonders of magic. If one were a fairy and knew the secret laws of nature and the mystic words and ceremonies

that commanded those laws, then a simple wave of a silver wand would produce instantly all that men work hard and anxiously for through weary years. And Dorothy wished in her kindly, innocent heart, that all men and women could be fairies with silver wands, and satisfy all their needs without so much work and worry, for then, she imagined, they would have all their working hours to be happy in. But Ozma, looking into her friend's face and reading those thoughts, gave a laugh and said:

'No, no, Dorothy, that wouldn't do at all. Instead of happiness your plan would bring weariness to the world. If everyone could wave a wand and have his wants fulfilled there would be little to wish for. There would be no eager striving to obtain the difficult, for nothing would then be difficult, and the pleasure of earning something longed for, and only to be secured by hard work and careful thought, would be utterly lost. There would be nothing to do, you see, and no interest in life and in our fellow creatures. That is all that makes life worth our while – to do good deeds and to help those less fortunate than ourselves.'

'Well, you're a fairy, Ozma. Aren't you happy?' asked Dorothy.

'Yes, dear, because I can use my fairy powers to make others happy. Had I no kingdom to rule, and no subjects to look after, I would be miserable. Also, you must realize that while I am a more powerful fairy than any other inhabitant of Oz, I am not as powerful as Glinda the Sorceress, who has studied many arts of magic that I know nothing of. Even the little Wizard of Oz can do some things I am unable to accomplish, while I can accomplish things unknown to the Wizard. This is to explain that I am not all-powerful, by any means. My magic is simply fairy magic, and not sorcery or wizardry.'

'All the same,' said Dorothy, 'I'm mighty glad you could make this tent appear, with our dinners and beds all ready for us.'

Ozma smiled.

'Yes, it is indeed wonderful,' she agreed. 'Not all fairies know that sort of magic, but some fairies can do magic that fills me with astonishment. I think that is what makes us modest and unassuming – the fact that our magic arts are divided, some being given each of us. I'm glad I don't know everything, Dorothy, and that there still are things in both nature and in wit for me to marvel at.'

Dorothy couldn't quite understand this, so she said nothing more on the subject and presently had a new reason to marvel. For when they had quite finished their meal table and contents disappeared in a flash.

'No dishes to wash, Ozma!' she said with a laugh. 'I guess you'd make a lot of folks happy if you could teach 'em just that one trick.'

For an hour Ozma told stories, and talked with Dorothy about various people in whom they were interested. And then it was bedtime, and they undressed and crept into their soft beds and fell asleep almost as soon as their heads touched their pillows.

5

The Magic Stairway

THE flat mountain looked much nearer in the clear light of the morning sun, but Dorothy and Ozma knew there was a long tramp before them, even yet. They finished dressing only to find a warm, delicious breakfast awaiting them, and having eaten they left the tent and started toward the mountain which was their first goal. After going a little way Dorothy looked back and found that the fairy tent had entirely disappeared. She was not surprised, for she knew this would happen.

'Can't your magic give us a horse an' wagon, or an automobile?' inquired Dorothy.

'No, dear; I'm sorry that such magic is beyond my power,' confessed her fairy friend.

'Perhaps Glinda could,' said Dorothy thoughtfully.

'Glinda has a stork chariot that carries her through the air,' said Ozma, 'but even our great Sorceress cannot conjure up other modes of travel. Don't forget what I told you last night, that no one is powerful enough to do everything.'

'Well, I s'pose I ought to know that, having lived so long in the Land of Oz,' replied Dorothy; 'but I can't do any magic at all, an' so I can't figure out e'zactly how you an' Glinda an' the Wizard do it.'

'Don't try,' laughed Ozma. 'But you have at least one magical art, Dorothy: you know the trick of winning all hearts.'

'No, I don't,' said Dorothy earnestly. 'If I really can do it, Ozma, I am sure I don't know *how* I do it.'

It took them a good two hours to reach the foot of the round, flat mountain, and then they found the sides so steep that they were like the wall of a house.

'Even my purple kitten couldn't climb 'em,' remarked Dorothy, gazing upward.

'But there is some way for the Flatheads to get down and up again,' declared Ozma; 'otherwise they couldn't make war with the Skeezers, or even meet them and quarrel with them.'

'That's so, Ozma. Let's walk around a ways; perhaps we'll find a ladder or something.'

They walked quite a distance, for it was a big mountain, and as they circled around it and came to the side that faced the palm trees, they suddenly discovered an entrance way cut out of the rock wall. This entrance was arched overhead and not very deep because it merely led to a short flight of stone stairs.

'Oh, we've found a way to the top at last,' announced Ozma, and the two girls turned and walked straight toward the entrance. Suddenly they bumped against something and stood still, unable to proceed farther.

'Dear me!' exclaimed Dorothy, rubbing her nose, which had struck something hard, although she could not see what it was; 'this isn't as easy as it looks. What has stopped us, Ozma? Is it magic of some sort?'

Ozma was feeling around, her hands outstretched before her.

'Yes, dear, it is magic,' she replied. 'The Flatheads had to have a way from their mountain top from the plain below, but to prevent enemies from rushing up the stairs to conquer them, they have built at a small distance before the entrance a wall of solid stone, the stones being held in place by cement, and then they made the wall invisible.'

'I wonder why they did that?' mused Dorothy. 'A wall

would keep folks out anyhow, whether it could be seen or not, so there wasn't any use making it invisible. Seems to me it would have been better to have left it solid, for then no one would have seen the entrance behind it. Now anybody can see the entrance, as we did. And prob'bly anybody that tries to go up the stairs gets bumped, as we did.'

Ozma made no reply at once. Her face was grave and thoughtful.

'I think I know the reason for making the wall invisible,' she said after a while. 'The Flatheads use the stairs for coming down and going up. If there was a solid stone wall to keep them from reaching the plain they would themselves be imprisoned by the wall. So they had to leave some place to get round the wall, and, if the wall was visible, all strangers or enemies would find the place to go round it and then the wall would be useless. So the Flatheads cunningly made their wall invisible, believing that everyone who saw the entrance to the mountain would walk straight toward it, as we did, and find it impossible to go any farther. I suppose the wall is really high and thick, and can't be broken through, so those who find it in their way are obliged to go away again.'

'Well,' said Dorothy, 'if there's a way round the wall, where is it?'

'We must find it,' returned Ozma, and began feeling her way along the wall. Dorothy followed and began to get discouraged when Ozma had walked nearly a quarter of a mile away from the entrance. But now the invisible wall curved in toward the side of the mountain and suddenly ended, leaving just space enough between the wall and the mountain for an ordinary person to pass through.

The girls went in, single file, and Ozma explained that they were now behind the barrier and could go back to the entrance. They met no further obstructions.

'Most people, Ozma, wouldn't have figured this thing out the way you did,' remarked Dorothy. 'If I'd been alone the invisible wall surely would have stumped me.'

Reaching the entrance they began to mount the stone stairs. They went up ten stairs and then down five stairs, following a passage cut from the rock. The stairs were just wide enough for the two girls to walk abreast, arm in arm. At the bottom of the five stairs the passage turned to the right, and they ascended ten more stairs, only to find at the top of the flight five stairs leading straight down again. Again the passage turned abruptly, this time to the left, and then more stairs led upward.

The passage was now quite dark, for they were in the heart of the mountain and all daylight had been shut out by the turns of the passage. However, Ozma drew her silver wand from her bosom and the great jewel at its end gave out a lustrous, green-tinted light which lighted the place well enough for them to see their way plainly.

Ten steps up, five steps down, and a turn, this way or that. That was the programme, and Dorothy figured that they were only gaining five stairs upward each trip that they made.

'Those Flatheads must be funny people,' she said to Ozma. 'They don't seem to do anything in a bold, straight-forward manner. In making this passage they forced every-one to walk three times as far as is necessary. And of course this trip is just as tiresome to the Flatheads as it is to other folks.'

'That is true,' answered Ozma; 'yet it is a clever arrange-ment to prevent their being surprised by intruders. Every time we reach the tenth step of a flight, the pressure of our feet on the stone makes a bell ring on top of the mountain, to warn the Flatheads of our coming.'

'How do you know that?' demanded Dorothy, astonished.

'I've heard the bell ever since we started,' Ozma told her. 'You could not hear it, I know, but when I am holding my wand in my hand I can hear sounds a great distance off.'

'Do you hear anything on top of the mountain 'cept the bell?' inquired Dorothy.

'Yes. The people are calling to one another in alarm and many footsteps are approaching the place where we will reach the flat top of the mountain.'

This made Dorothy feel somewhat anxious.

'I'd thought we were going to visit just common, ordinary people,' she remarked, 'but they're pretty clever, it seems, and they know some kinds of magic, too. They may be dangerous, Ozma. P'raps we'd better stayed at home.'

Finally the upstairs-and-downstairs passage seemed coming to an end, for daylight again appeared ahead of the two girls and Ozma replaced her wand in the bosom of her gown. The last ten steps brought them to the surface, where they found themselves surrounded by such a throng of queer people that for a time they halted, speechless, and stared into the faces that confronted them.

Dorothy knew at once why these mountain people were called Flatheads. Their heads were really flat on top, as if they had been cut off just above the eyes and ears. Also the heads were bald, with no hair on top at all, and the ears were big and stuck straight out, and the noses were small and stubby, while the mouths of the Flatheads were well shaped and not unusual. Their eyes were perhaps their best feature, being large and bright and a deep violet in colour.

The costumes of the Flatheads were all made of metals dug from their mountain. Small gold, silver, tin and iron discs, about the size of pennies, and very thin, were cleverly wired together and made to form knee trousers and jackets for the men and skirts and blouses for the women. The coloured metals were skilfully mixed to form stripes and checks of various sorts, so that the costumes were quite gorgeous and reminded Dorothy of pictures she had seen of Knights of old clothed in armour.

Aside from their flat heads, these people were not really bad looking. The men were armed with bows and arrows and had small axes of steel stuck in their metal belts. They wore no hats nor ornaments.

6

Flathead Mountain

WHEN they saw that the intruders on their mountain were only two little girls, the Flatheads grunted with satisfaction and drew back, permitting them to see what the mountain top looked like. It was shaped like a saucer, so that the houses and other buildings – all made of rocks – could not be seen over the edge by anyone standing in the plain below.

But now a big fat Flathead stood before the girls and in a gruff voice demanded:

'What are you doing here? Have the Skeezers sent you to spy upon us?'

'I am Princess Ozma, Ruler of all the Land of Oz.'

'Well, I've never heard of the Land of Oz, so you may be what you claim,' returned the Flathead.

'This is the Land of Oz – part of it, anyway,' exclaimed Dorothy. 'So Princess Ozma rules you Flathead people, as well as all the other people in Oz.'

The man laughed, and all the others who stood around laughed, too. Some one in the crowd called:

'She'd better not tell the Supreme Dictator about ruling the Flatheads. Eh, friends?'

'No, indeed!' they all answered in positive tones.

'Who is your Supreme Dictator?' asked Ozma.

'I think I'll let him tell you that himself,' answered the man who had first spoken. 'You have broken our laws by coming here; and whoever you are the Supreme Dictator must fix your punishment. Come along with me.'

He started down a path and Ozma and Dorothy followed

him without protest, as they wanted to see the most important person in this queer country. The houses they passed seemed pleasant enough and each had a little yard in which were flowers and vegetables. Walls of rock separated the dwellings, and all the paths were paved with smooth slabs of rock. This seemed their only building material and they utilized it cleverly for every purpose.

Directly in the centre of the great saucer stood a larger building which the Flathead informed the girls was the palace of the Supreme Dictator. He led them through an entrance hall into a big reception room, where they sat upon stone benches and awaited the coming of the Dictator. Pretty soon he entered from another room – a rather lean and rather old Flathead, dressed much like the others of this strange race, and only distinguished from them by the sly and cunning expression of his face. He kept his eyes half closed and looked through the slits of them at Ozma and Dorothy, who rose to receive him.

'Are you the Supreme Dictator of the Flatheads?' inquired Ozma.

'Yes, that's me,' he said, rubbing his hands slowly together. 'My word is law. I'm the head of the Flatheads on this flat headland.'

'I am Princess Ozma of Oz, and I have come from the Emerald City to—'

'Stop a minute,' interrupted the Dictator, and turned to the man who had brought the girls there. 'Go away, Dictator Felo Flathead!' he commanded. 'Return to your duty and guard the Stairway. I will look after these strangers.' The man bowed and departed, and Dorothy asked wonderingly:

'Is *he* a Dictator, too?'

'Of course,' was the answer. 'Everybody here is a dictator of something or other. They're all office holders. That's what keeps them contented. But I'm the Supreme Dictator of all, and I'm elected once a year. This is a democracy, you know, where the people are allowed to vote for their rulers. A good many others would like to be Supreme Dictator, but as I made a law that I am always to count the votes myself, I am always elected.'

'What is your name?' asked Ozma.

'I am called the Su-dic, which is short for Supreme Dictator. I sent that man away because the moment you mentioned Ozma of Oz, and the Emerald City, I knew who you were. I suppose I'm the only Flathead that ever heard of you, but that's because I have more brains than the rest.'

Dorothy was staring hard at the Su-dic.

'I don't see how you can have any brains at all,' she remarked, 'because the part of your head is gone where brains are kept.'

'I don't blame you for thinking that,' he said. 'Once the Flatheads had no brains because, as you say, there is no upper part to their heads, to hold brains. But long, long ago a band of fairies flew over this country and made it all a fairyland, and when they came to the Flatheads the fairies were sorry to find them all very stupid and quite unable to think. So as there was no good place in their bodies in which to put brains the Fairy Queen gave each one of us a nice can of brains to carry in his pocket and that made us just as intelligent as other people. See,' he continued, 'here is one of the cans of brains the fairies gave us.' He took from a pocket a bright tin can having a pretty red label on it which said: 'Flathead Concentrated Brains, Extra Quality.'

'And does every Flathead have the same kind of brains?' asked Dorothy.

'Yes, they're all alike. Here's another can.' From another pocket he produced a second can of brains.

'Did the fairies give you a double supply?' inquired Dorothy.

'No, but one of the Flatheads thought he wanted to be the Su-dic and tried to get my people to rebel against me, so I punished him by taking away his brains. One day my wife scolded me severely, so I took away her can of brains. She didn't like that and went out and robbed several women of *their* brains. Then I made a law that if anyone stole another's brains, or even tried to borrow them, he would forfeit his own brains to the Su-dic. So each one is content with his own canned brains and my wife and I are the only ones on the mountain with more than one can. I have three cans and that makes me very clever – so clever that I'm a good Sorcerer, if I do say it myself. My poor wife had four cans of brains and became a remarkable witch, but alas! that was before those terrible enemies, the Skeezers, transformed her into a Golden Pig.'

'Good gracious!' cried Dorothy; 'is your wife really **a** Golden Pig?'

'She is. The Skeezers did it and so I have declared war on
them. In revenge for making my wife a Pig I intend to ruin
their Magic Island and make the Skeezers the slaves of the
Flatheads!'

The Su-dic was very angry now; his eyes flashed and his
face took on a wicked and fierce expression. But Ozma said
to him, very sweetly and in a friendly voice:

'I am sorry to hear this. Will you please tell me more
about your troubles with the Skeezers? Then perhaps I can
help you.'

She was only a girl, but there was dignity in her pose and
speech which impressed the Su-dic.

'If you are really Princess Ozma of Oz,' the Flathead
said, 'you are one of that band of fairies who, under Queen
Lurline, made all Oz a Fairyland. I have heard that Lurline
left one of her own fairies to rule Oz, and gave the fairy the
name of Ozma.'

'If you knew this why did you not come to me at the
Emerald City and tender me your loyalty and obedience?'
asked the Ruler of Oz.

'Well, I only learned the fact lately, and I've been too
busy to leave home,' he explained, looking at the floor instead
of into Ozma's eyes. She knew he had spoken a falsehood,
but only said:

'Why did you quarrel with the Skeezers?'

'It was this way,' began the Su-dic, glad to change the
subject. 'We Flatheads love fish, and as we have no fish on
this mountain we would sometimes go to the Lake of the
Skeezers to catch fish. This made the Skeezers angry, for
they declared the fish in their lake belonged to them and
were under their protection and they forbade us to catch
them. That was very mean and unfriendly in the Skeezers,
you must admit, and when we paid no attention to their

orders they set a guard on the shore of the lake to prevent our fishing.

'Now, my wife, Rora Flathead, having four cans of brains, had become a wonderful witch, and fish being brain food, she loved to eat fish better than any one of us. So she vowed she would destroy every fish in the lake, unless the Skeezers let us catch what we wanted. They defied us, so Rora prepared a kettleful of magic poison and went down to the lake one night to dump it all in the water and poison the fish. It was a clever idea, quite worthy of my dear wife, but the Skeezer Queen – a young lady named Coo-ee-oh – hid on the bank of the lake and taking Rora unawares, transformed her into a Golden Pig. The poison was spilled on the ground and wicked Queen Coo-ee-oh, not content with her cruel transformation, even took away my wife's four cans of brains, so she is now a common grunting pig without even brains enough to know her own name.'

'Then,' said Ozma thoughtfully, 'the Queen of the Skeezers must be a Sorceress.'

'Yes,' said the Su-dic, 'but she doesn't know much magic, after all. She is not as powerful as Rora Flathead was, nor half as powerful as I am now, as Queen Coo-ee-oh will discover when we fight our great battle and destroy her.'

'The Golden Pig can't be a witch any more, of course,' observed Dorothy.

'No; even had Queen Coo-ee-oh left her the four cans of brains, poor Rora, in a pig's shape, couldn't do any witchcraft. A witch has to use her fingers, and a pig has only cloven hoofs.'

'It seems a sad story,' was Ozma's comment, 'and all the trouble arose because the Flatheads wanted fish that did not belong to them.'

'As for that,' said the Su-dic, again angry, 'I made a law that any of my people could catch fish in the Lake of the

Skeezers, whenever they wanted to. So the trouble was through the Skeezers defying my law.'

'You can only make laws to govern your own people,' asserted Ozma sternly. 'I, alone, am empowered to make laws that must be obeyed by all the peoples of Oz.'

'Pooh!' cried the Su-dic scornfully. 'You can't make *me* obey your laws, I assure you. I know the extent of your powers, Princess Ozma of Oz, and I know that I am more powerful than you are. To prove it I shall keep you and your companion prisoners in this mountain until after we have fought and conquered the Skeezers. Then, if you promise to be good, I may let you go home again.'

Dorothy was amazed by this effrontery and defiance of the beautiful girl Ruler of Oz, whom all until now had obeyed without question. But Ozma, still unruffled and dignified, looked at the Su-dic and said:

'You did not mean that. You are angry and speak unwisely, without reflection. I came here from my palace in the Emerald City to prevent war and to make peace between you and the Skeezers. I do not approve of Queen Coo-ee-oh's action in transforming your wife Rora into a pig, nor do I approve of Rora's cruel attempt to poison the fishes in the lake. No one has the right to work magic in my dominions without my consent, so the Flatheads and the Skeezers have both broken my laws – which must be obeyed.'

'If you want to make peace,' said the Su-dic, 'make the Skeezers restore my wife to her proper form and give back her four cans of brains. Also make them agree to allow us to catch fish in their lake.'

'No,' returned Ozma, 'I will not do that, for it would be unjust. I will have the Golden Pig again transformed into your wife Rora, and give her one can of brains, but the other three cans must be restored to those she robbed. Neither may you catch fish in the Lake of the Skeezers, for it is their lake and the fish belong to them. This arrangement is just and honourable, and you must agree to it.'

'Never!' cried the Su-dic. Just then a pig came running into the room, uttering dismal grunts. It was made of solid gold, with joints at the bends of the legs and in the neck and jaws. The Golden Pig's eyes were rubies, and its teeth were polished ivory.

'There!' said the Su-dic, 'gaze on the evil work of Queen Coo-ee-oh, and then say if you can prevent my making war on the Skeezers. That grunting beast was once my wife – the most beautiful Flathead on our mountain and a skilful witch. Now look at her!'

'Fight the Skeezers, fight the Skeezers, fight the Skeezers!' grunted the Golden Pig.

'I *will* fight the Skeezers,' exclaimed the Flathead chief, 'and if a dozen Ozmas of Oz forbade me I would fight just the same.'

'Not if I can prevent it!' asserted Ozma.

'You can't prevent it. But since you threaten me, I'll have you confined in the bronze prison until the war is over,' said the Su-dic. He whistled and four stout Flatheads, armed with axes and spears, entered the room and saluted him. Turning to the men he said: 'Take these two girls, bind them with wire ropes and cast them into the bronze prison.'

The four men bowed low and one of them asked:

'Where are the two girls, most noble Su-dic?'

The Su-dic turned to where Ozma and Dorothy had stood but they had vanished!

7

The Magic Isle

Ozma, seeing it was useless to argue with the Supreme Dictator of the Flatheads, had been considering how best to escape from his power. She realized that his sorcery might be difficult to overcome, and when he threatened to cast Dorothy and her into a bronze prison she slipped her hand into her bosom and grasped her silver wand. With the other hand she grasped the hand of Dorothy, but these motions were so natural that the Su-dic did not notice them. Then when he turned to meet his four soldiers, Ozma instantly rendered both herself and Dorothy invisible and swiftly led her companion around the group of Flatheads and out of the room. As they reached the entry and descended the stone steps, Ozma whispered:

'Let us run, dear! We are invisible, so no one will see us.'

Dorothy understood and she was a good runner. Ozma had marked the place where the grand stairway that led to the plain was located, so they made directly for it. Some people were in the paths but these they dodged around. One or two Flatheads heard the pattering of footsteps of the girls on the stone pavement and stopped with bewildered looks to gaze around them, but no one interfered with the invisible fugitives.

The Su-dic had lost no time in starting the chase. He and his men ran so fast that they might have overtaken the girls before they reached the stairway had not the Golden Pig suddenly run across their path. The Su-dic tripped over the pig and fell flat, and his four men tripped over him and tumbled in a heap. Before they could scramble up and reach the mouth of the passage it was too late to stop the two girls.

There was a guard on each side of the stairway, but of course they did not see Ozma and Dorothy as they sped past and descended the steps. Then they had to go up five steps and down another ten, and so on, in the same manner in which they had climbed to the top of the mountain. Ozma lighted their way with her wand and they kept on without relaxing their speed until they reached the bottom. Then they ran to the right and turned the corner of the invisible wall just as the Su-dic and his followers rushed out of the arched entrance and looked around in an attempt to discover the fugitives.

Ozma now knew they were safe, so she told Dorothy to stop and both of them sat down on the grass until they could breathe freely and become rested from their mad flight.

As for the Su-dic, he realized he was foiled and soon turned and climbed his stairs again. He was very angry – angry with Ozma and angry with himself – because, now that he took time to think, he remembered that he knew very well the art of making people invisible, and visible again, and if he had only thought of it in time he could have used his magic knowledge to make the girls visible and so have captured them easily. However, it was now too late for regrets and he determined to make preparations at once to march all his forces against the Skeezers.

'What shall we do next?' asked Dorothy, when they were rested.

'Let us find the Lake of the Skeezers,' replied Ozma. 'From what that dreadful Su-dic said I imagine the Skeezers are good people and worthy of our friendship, and if we go to them we may help them to defeat the Flatheads.'

'I s'pose we can't stop the war now,' remarked Dorothy reflectively, as they walked toward the row of palm trees.

'No; the Su-dic is determined to fight the Skeezers, so all we can do is to warn them of their danger and help them as much as possible.'

'Of course you'll punish the Flatheads,' said Dorothy.

'Well, I do not think the Flathead people are as much to blame as their Supreme Dictator,' was the answer. 'If he is removed from power and his unlawful magic taken from him, the people will probably be good and respect the laws of the Land of Oz, and live at peace with all their neighbours in the future.'

'I hope so,' said Dorothy with a sigh of doubt.

The palms were not far from the mountain and the girls reached them after a brisk walk. The huge trees were set close together, in three rows, and had been planted so as to keep people from passing them, but the Flatheads had cut a passage through this barrier and Ozma found the path and led Dorothy to the other side.

Beyond the palms they discovered a very beautiful scene. Bordered by a green lawn was a great lake fully a mile from shore to shore, the waters of which were exquisitely blue and sparkling, with little wavelets breaking its smooth surface where the breezes touched it. In the centre of this lake appeared a lovely island, not of great extent but almost entirely covered by a huge round building with glass walls and a high glass dome which glittered brilliantly in the sunshine. Between the glass building and the edge of the island was no grass, flowers or shrubbery, but only an expanse of highly polished white marble. There were no boats on either shore and no signs of life could be seen anywhere on the island.

'Well,' said Dorothy, gazing wistfully at the island, 'we've found the Lake of the Skeezers and their Magic Isle. I guess the Skeezers are in that big glass palace, but we can't get at 'em."

8

Queen Coo-ee-oh

PRINCESS OZMA considered the situation gravely. Then she tied her handkerchief to her wand and, standing at the water's edge, waved the handkerchief like a flag, as a signal. For a time they could observe no response.

'I don't see what good that will do,' said Dorothy. 'Even if the Skeezers are on that island and see us, and know we're friends, they haven't any boats to come and get us.'

But the Skeezers didn't need boats, as the girls soon discovered. For on a sudden an opening appeared at the base of the palace and from the opening came a slender shaft of steel, reaching out slowly but steadily across the water in the direction of the place where they stood. To the girls this steel arrangement looked like a triangle, with the base nearest the water. It came toward them in the form of an arch, stretching out from the palace wall until its end reached the bank and rested there, while the other end still remained on the island.

Then they saw that it was a bridge, consisting of a steel footway just broad enough to walk on, and two slender guide rails, one on either side, which were connected with the footway by steel bars. The bridge looked rather frail and Dorothy feared it would not bear their weight, but Ozma at once called, 'Come on!' and started to walk across, holding fast to the rail on either side. So Dorothy summoned her courage and followed after. Before Ozma had taken three steps she halted and so forced Dorothy to halt, for the bridge was again moving and returning to the island.

'We need not walk after all,' said Ozma. So they stood still in their places and let the steel bridge draw them onward. Indeed, the bridge drew them well into the glass-domed building which covered the island, and soon they found themselves standing in a marble room where two handsomely dressed young men stood on a platform to receive them.

Ozma at once stepped from the end of the bridge to the marble platform, followed by Dorothy, and then the bridge disappeared with a slight clang of steel and a marble slab covered the opening from which it had emerged.

The two young men bowed profoundly to Ozma, and one of them said:

'Queen Coo-ee-oh bids you welcome, O Strangers. Her Majesty is waiting to receive you in her palace.'

'Lead on,' replied Ozma with dignity.

But instead of 'leading on', the platform of marble began to rise, carrying them upward through a square hole above which just fitted it. A moment later they found themselves within the great glass dome that covered almost all of the island.

Within this dome was a little village, with houses, streets, gardens and parks. The houses were of coloured marbles, prettily designed, with many stained-glass windows, and the streets and gardens seemed well cared for. Exactly under the centre of the lofty dome was a small park filled with brilliant flowers, with an elaborate fountain, and facing this park stood a building larger and more imposing than the others. Toward this building the young men escorted Ozma and Dorothy.

On the streets and in the doorways or open windows of the houses were men, women and children, all richly dressed. These were much like other people in different parts of the Land of Oz, except that instead of seeming merry and contented they all wore expressions of much solemnity or of nervous irritation. They had beautiful homes, splendid clothes, and ample food, but Dorothy at once decided something was wrong with their lives and that they were not happy. She said nothing, however, but looked curiously at the Skeezers.

At the entrance of the palace Ozma and Dorothy were met by two other young men, in uniform and armed with queer weapons that seemed about half-way between pistols and guns, but were like neither. Their conductors bowed and left them, and the two in uniforms led the girls into the palace.

In a beautiful throne room, surrounded by a dozen or more young men and women, sat the Queen of the Skeezers, Coo-ee-oh. She was a girl who looked older than Ozma or Dorothy – fifteen or sixteen, at least – and although she was elaborately dressed as if she were going to a ball she was too thin and plain of feature to be pretty. But evidently Queen Coo-ee-oh did not realize this fact, for her air and manner betrayed her as proud and haughty and with a high regard for her own importance. Dorothy at once decided she was 'snippy' and that she would not like Queen Coo-ee-oh as a companion.

The Queen's hair was as black as her skin was white and her eyes were black, too. The eyes, as she calmly examined Ozma and Dorothy, had a suspicious and unfriendly look in them, but she said quietly:

'I know who you are, for I have consulted my Magic Oracle, which told me that one calls herself Princess Ozma, the Ruler of all the Land of Oz, and the other is Princess Dorothy of Oz, who came from a country called Kansas. I know nothing of the Land of Oz, and I know nothing of Kansas.'

'Why, *this* is the Land of Oz!' cried Dorothy. 'It's a

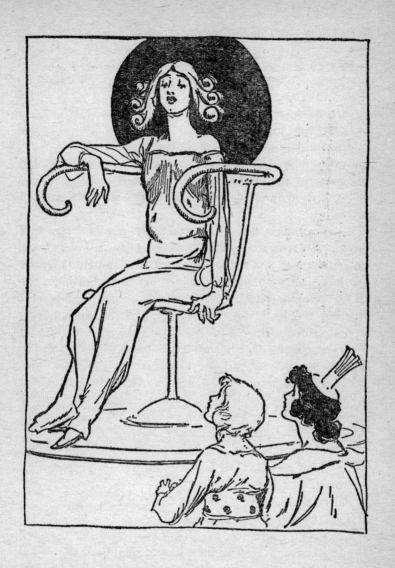

part of the Land of Oz, anyhow, whether you know it or not.'

'Oh, in-deed!' answered Queen Coo-ee-oh, scornfully. 'I suppose you will claim next that this Princess Ozma, ruling the Land of Oz, rules me!'

'Of course,' returned Dorothy. 'There's no doubt of it.'

The Queen turned to Ozma.

'Do you dare make such a claim?' she asked.

By this time Ozma had made up her mind as to the character of this haughty and disdainful creature, whose self-pride evidently led her to believe herself superior to all others.

'I did not come here to quarrel with your Majesty,' said the girl Ruler of Oz, quietly. 'What and who I am is well established, and my authority comes from the Fairy Queen Lurline, of whose band I was a member when Lurline made all Oz a Fairyland. There are several countries and several different peoples in this broad land, each of which has its separate rulers, Kings, Emperors and Queens. But all these render obedience to my laws and acknowledge me as the supreme Ruler.'

'If other Kings and Queens are fools that does not interest me in the least,' replied Coo-ee-oh, disdainfully. 'In the Land of the Skeezers I alone am supreme. You are impudent to think I would defer to you – or to anyone else.'

'Let us not speak of this now, please,' answered Ozma. 'Your island is in danger, for a powerful foe is preparing to destroy it.'

'Pah! The Flatheads. I do not fear them.'

'Their Supreme Dictator is a Sorcerer.'

'My magic is greater than his. Let the Flatheads come! They will never return to their barren mountain-top. I will see to that.'

Ozma did not like this attitude, for it meant that the Skeezers were eager to fight the Flatheads, and Ozma's object in coming here was to prevent fighting and induce the two quarrelsome neighbours to make peace. She was also greatly disappointed in Coo-ee-oh, for the reports of Su-dic had led her to imagine the Queen more just and honourable than were the Flatheads. Indeed Ozma reflected that the girl might be better at heart than her self-pride and overbearing manner indicated, and in any event it would be wise not to antagonize her but to try to win her friendship.

'I do not like wars, your Majesty,' said Ozma. 'In the Emerald City, where I rule thousands of people, and in the countries near to the Emerald City, where thousands more acknowledge my rule, there is no army at all, because there is no quarrelling and no need to fight. If differences arise between my people, they come to me and I judge the cases and award justice to all. So, when I learned there might be war between two far away people of Oz, I came here to settle the dispute and adjust the quarrel.'

'No one asked you to come,' declared Queen Coo-ee-oh. 'It is *my* business to settle this dispute, not yours. You say my island is a part of the Land of Oz, which you rule, but that is all nonsense, for I've never heard of the Land of Oz, nor of you. You say you are a fairy, and that fairies gave you command over me. I don't believe it! What I *do* believe is that you are an impostor and have come here to stir up trouble among my people, who are already becoming difficult to manage. You two girls may even be spies of the vile Flatheads, for all I know, and may be trying to trick me. But understand this,' she added, proudly rising from her jewelled throne to confront them, 'I have magic powers greater than any fairy possesses, and greater than any Flathead possesses. I am a Krumbic Witch — the only

Krumbic Witch in the world – and I fear the magic of no other creature that exists! You say you rule thousands. I rule one hundred and one Skeezers. But every one of them trembles at my word. Now that Ozma of Oz and Princess Dorothy are here, I shall rule one hundred and three subjects, for you also shall bow before my power. More than that, in ruling you I also rule the thousands you say you rule.'

Dorothy was very indignant at this speech.

'I've got a pink kitten that sometimes talks like that,' she said, 'but after I give her a good whipping she doesn't think she's so high and mighty after all. If you only knew who Ozma is you'd be scared to death to talk to her like that!'

Queen Coo-ee-oh gave the girl a supercilious look. Then she turned again to Ozma.

'I happen to know,' said she, 'that the Flatheads intend to attack us tomorrow, but we are ready for them. Until the battle is over, I shall keep you two strangers prisoners on my island, from which there is no chance for you to escape.'

She turned and looked around the band of courtiers who stood silently around her throne.

'Lady Aurex,' she continued, singling out one of the young women, 'take these children to your house and care for them, giving them food and lodging. You may allow them to wander anywhere under the Great Dome, for they are harmless. After I have attended to the Flatheads I will consider what next to do with these foolish girls.'

She resumed her seat and the Lady Aurex bowed low and said in a humble manner:

'I obey your Majesty's commands.' Then to Ozma and Dorothy, she added 'Follow me', and turned to leave the throne room.

Dorothy looked to see what Ozma would do. To her

surprise and a little to her disappointment Ozma turned and followed Lady Aurex. So Dorothy trailed after them,but not without giving a parting, haughty look toward Queen Coo-ee-oh, who had her face turned the other way and did not see the disapproving look.

9

Lady Aurex

LADY AUREX led Ozma and Dorothy along a street to a pretty marble house near to one edge of the great glass dome that covered the village. She did not speak to the girls until she had ushered them into a pleasant room, comfortably furnished, nor did any of the solemn people they met on the street venture to speak.

When they were seated Lady Aurex asked if they were hungry, and finding they were summoned a maid and ordered food to be brought.

This Lady Aurex looked to be about twenty years old, although in the Land of Oz where people have never changed in appearance since the fairies made it a fairyland – where no one grows old or dies – it is always difficult to say how many years anyone has lived. She had a pleasant, attractive face, even though it was solemn and sad as the faces of all Skeezers seemed to be, and her costume was rich and elaborate, as became a lady in waiting upon the Queen.

Ozma had observed Lady Aurex closely and now asked her in a gentle tone:

'Do you, also, believe me to be an impostor?'

'I dare not say,' replied Lady Aurex in a low tone.

'Why are you afraid to speak freely?' inquired Ozma.

'The Queen punishes us if we make remarks that she does not like.'

'Are we not alone then, in this house?'

'The Queen can hear everything that is spoken on this

island – even the slightest whisper,' declared Lady Aurex.
'She is a wonderful witch, as she has told you, and it is folly
to criticize her or disobey her commands.'

Ozma looked into her eyes and saw that she would like
to say more if she dared. So she drew from her bosom her
silver wand, and having muttered a magic phrase in a
strange tongue, she left the room and walked slowly around
the outside of the house, making a complete circle and
waving her wand in mystic curves as she walked. Lady Aurex
watched her curiously and, when Ozma had again entered
the room and seated herself, she asked:

'What have you done?'

'I've enchanted this house in such a manner that Queen
Coo-ee-oh, with all her witchcraft, cannot hear one word
we speak within the magic circle I have made,' replied
Ozma. 'We may now speak freely and as loudly as we wish,
without fear of the Queen's anger.'

Lady Aurex brightened at this.

'Can I trust you?' she asked.

'Ev'rybody trusts Ozma,' exclaimed Dorothy. 'She is
true and honest, and your wicked Queen will be sorry she
insulted the powerful Ruler of all the Land of Oz.'

'The Queen does not know me yet,' said Ozma, 'but I
want you to know me, Lady Aurex, and I want you to tell
me why you, and all the Skeezers, are unhappy. Do not
fear Coo-ee-oh's anger, for she cannot hear a word we say,
I assure you.'

Lady Aurex was thoughtful a moment; then she said: 'I
shall trust you, Princess Ozma, for I believe you are what
you say you are – our supreme Ruler. If you knew the
dreadful punishments our Queen inflicts upon us, you
would not wonder we are so unhappy. The Skeezers are
not bad people; they do not care to quarrel and fight, even
with their enemies the Flatheads; but they are so cowed and

fearful of Coo-ee-oh that they obey her slightest word, rather than suffer her anger.'

'Hasn't she any heart, then?' asked Dorothy.

'She never displays mercy. She loves no one but herself,' asserted Lady Aurex, but she trembled as she said it, as if afraid even yet of her terrible Queen.

'That's pretty bad,' said Dorothy, shaking her head gravely. 'I see you've a lot to do here, Ozma, in this for-saken corner of the Land of Oz. First place, you've got to take the magic away from Queen Coo-ee-oh, and from that awful Su-dic, too. *My* idea is that neither of them is fit to rule anybody, 'cause they're cruel and hateful. So you'll have to give the Skeezers and Flatheads new rulers and teach all their people that they're part of the Land of Oz and must obey, above all, the lawful Ruler, Ozma of Oz. Then, when you've done that, we can go back home again.'

Ozma smiled at her little friend's earnest counsel, but Lady Aurex said in an anxious tone:

'I am surprised that you suggest these reforms while you are yet prisoners on this island and in Coo-ee-oh's power. That these things should be done, there is no doubt, but just now a dreadful war is likely to break out, and frightful things may happen to us all. Our Queen has such conceit that she thinks she can overcome the Su-dic and his people, but it is said Su-dic's magic is very powerful, although not as great as that possessed by his wife Rora, before Coo-ee-oh trans-formed her into a Golden Pig.'

'I don't blame her very much for doing that,' remarked Dorothy, 'for the Flatheads were wicked to try to catch your beautiful fish and the Witch Rora wanted to poison all the fishes in the lake.'

'Do you know the reason?' asked the Lady Aurex.

'I don't s'pose there *was* any reason, 'cept just wicked-ness,' replied Dorothy.

'Tell us the reason,' said Ozma earnestly.

'Well, your Majesty, once – a long time ago – the Flatheads and the Skeezers were friendly. They visited our island and we visited their mountain, and everything was pleasant between the two peoples. At that time the Flatheads were ruled by three Adepts in Sorcery, beautiful girls who were not Flatheads, but had wandered to the Flat Mountain and made their home there. These three Adepts used their magic only for good, and the mountain people gladly made them their rulers. They taught the Flatheads how to use their canned brains and how to work metals into clothing that would never wear out, and many other things that added to their happiness and content.

'Coo-ee-oh was our Queen then, as now, but she knew no magic and so had nothing to be proud of. But the three Adepts were very kind to Coo-ee-oh. They built for us this wonderful dome of glass and our houses of marble and taught us to make beautiful clothing and many other things. Coo-ee-oh pretended to be very grateful for these favours, but it seems that all the time she was jealous of the three Adepts and secretly tried to discover their arts of magic. In this she was more clever than anyone suspected. She invited the three Adepts to a banquet one day, and while they were feasting Coo-ee-oh stole their charms and magical instruments and transformed them into three fishes – a gold fish, a silver fish and a bronze fish. While the poor fishes were gasping and flopping helplessly on the floor of the banquet room one of them said reproachfully: "You will be punished for this, Coo-ee-oh, for if one of us dies or is destroyed, you will become shrivelled and helpless, and all your stolen magic will depart from you." Frightened by this threat, Coo-ee-oh at once caught up the three fish and ran with them to the shore of the lake, where she cast them

into the water. This revived the three Adepts and they
swam away and disappeared.

'I myself, witnessed this shocking scene,' continued Lady
Aurex, 'and so did many other Skeezers. The news was
carried to the Flatheads, who then turned from friends to
enemies. The Su-dic and his wife Rora were the only ones
on the mountain who were glad the three Adepts had been
lost to them, and they at once became Rulers of the Flatheads and stole their canned brains from others to make
themselves the more powerful. Some of the Adepts' magic
tools had been left on the mountain, and these Rora seized
and by the use of them she became a witch.

'The result of Coo-ee-oh's treachery was to make both
the Skeezers and the Flatheads miserable instead of happy.
Not only were the Su-dic and his wife cruel to their people,
but our Queen at once became proud and arrogant and
treated us very unkindly. All the Skeezers knew she had
stolen her magic powers and so she hated us and made us
humble ourselves before her and obey her slightest word. If
we disobeyed, or did not please her, or if we talked about her
when we were in our own homes she would have us dragged
to the whipping post in her palace and lashed with knotted
cords. That is why we fear her so greatly.'

This story filled Ozma's heart with sorrow and Dorothy's
heart with indignation.

'I now understand,' said Ozma, 'why the fishes in the
lake have brought about war between the Skeezers and the
Flatheads.'

'Yes,' Lady Aurex answered, 'now that you know the
story it is easy to understand. The Su-dic and his wife came
to our lake hoping to catch the silver fish, or gold fish, or
bronze fish – any one of them *would* do – and by destroying
it deprive Coo-ee-oh of her magic. Then they could easily
conquer her. Also they had another reason for wanting to

catch the fish – they feared that in some way the three Adepts might regain their proper forms and then they would be sure to return to the mountain and punish Rora and the Su-dic. That was why Rora finally tried to poison all the fishes in the lake, at the time Coo-ee-oh transformed her into a Golden Pig. Of course this attempt to destroy the fishes frightened the Queen, for her safety lies in keeping the three fishes alive.'

'I s'pose Coo-ee-oh will fight the Flatheads with all her might,' observed Dorothy.

'And with all her magic,' added Ozma, thoughtfully.

'I do not see how the Flatheads can get to this island to hurt us,' said Lady Aurex.

'They have bows and arrows, and I guess they mean to shoot the arrows at your big dome, and break all the glass in it,' suggested Dorothy.

But Lady Aurex shook her head with a smile.

'They cannot do that,' she replied.

'Why not?'

'I dare not tell you why, but if the Flatheads come tomorrow morning you will yourselves see the reason.'

'I do not think they will attempt to harm the island,' Ozma declared. 'I believe they will first attempt to destroy the fishes, by poison or some other means. If they succeed in that, the conquest of the island will not be difficult.'

'They have no boats,' said Lady Aurex, 'and Coo-ee-oh, who has long expected this war, has been preparing for it in many astonishing ways. I almost wish the Flatheads would conquer us, for then we would be free from our dreadful Queen; but I do not wish to see the three transformed fishes destroyed, for in them lies our only hope of future happiness.'

'Ozma will take care of you, whatever happens,' Dorothy assured her. But the Lady Aurex, not knowing the extent of

Ozma's power – which was, in fact, not so great as Dorothy imagined – could not take much comfort in this promise.

It was evident there would be exciting times on the morrow, if the Flatheads really attacked the Skeezers of the Magic Isle.

Under Water

WHEN night fell all the interior of the Great Dome, streets and houses, became lighted with brilliant incandescent lamps, which rendered it bright as day. Dorothy thought the island must look beautiful by night from the outer shore of the lake. There was revelry and feasting in the Queen's palace, and the music of the royal band could be plainly heard in Lady Aurex's house, where Ozma and Dorothy remained with their hostess and keeper. They were prisoners, but treated with much consideration.

Lady Aurex gave them a nice supper and when they wished to retire showed them to a pretty room with comfortable beds and wished them a good night and pleasant dreams.

'What do you think of all this, Ozma?' Dorothy anxiously inquired when they were alone.

'I am glad we came,' was the reply, 'for although there may be mischief done tomorrow, it was necessary I should know about these people, whose leaders are wild and lawless and oppress their subjects with injustice and cruelties. My task, therefore, is to liberate the Skeezers and the Flatheads and secure for them freedom and happiness. I have no doubt I can accomplish this in time.'

'Just now, though, we're in a bad fix,' asserted Dorothy. 'If Queen Coo-ee-oh conquers tomorrow, she won't be nice to us, and if the Su-dic conquers, he'll be worse.'

'Do not worry, dear,' said Ozma, 'I do not think we are in danger, whatever happens, and the result of our adventure is sure to be good.'

Dorothy was not worrying, especially. She had confidence in her friend, the fairy Princess of Oz, and she enjoyed the excitement of the events in which she was taking part. So she crept into bed and fell asleep as easily as if she had been in her own cosy room in Ozma's palace.

A sort of grating, grinding sound awakened her. The whole island seemed to tremble and sway, as it might do in an earthquake. Dorothy sat up in bed, rubbing her eyes to get the sleep out of them, and then found it was daybreak.

Ozma was hurriedly dressing herself.

'What is it?' asked Dorothy, jumping out of bed.

'I'm not sure,' answered Ozma, 'but it feels as if the island is sinking.'

As soon as possible they finished dressing, while the creaking and swaying continued. Then they rushed into the living room of the house and found Lady Aurex, fully dressed, awaiting them.

'Do not be alarmed,' said their hostess. 'Coo-ee-oh has decided to submerge the island, that is all. But it proves the Flatheads are coming to attack us.'

'What do you mean by sub-sub-merging the island?' asked Dorothy.

'Come here and see,' was the reply.

Lady Aurex led them to a window which faced the side of the great dome which covered all the village, and they could see that the island was indeed sinking, for the water of the lake was already half-way up the side of the dome. Through the glass could be seen swimming fishes, and tall stalks of swaying seaweeds, for the water was clear as crystal and through it they could distinguish even the farther shore of the lake.

'The Flatheads are not here yet,' said Lady Aurex. 'They will come soon, but not until all of this dome is under the surface of the water.'

'Won't the dome leak?' Dorothy inquired anxiously.

'No, indeed.'

'Was the island ever sub-sub-sunk before?'

'Oh, yes; on several occasions. But Coo-ee-oh doesn't care to do that often, for it requires a lot of hard work to operate the machinery. The dome was built so that the island could disappear. I think,' she continued, 'that our Queen fears the Flatheads will attack the island and try to break the glass of the dome.'

'Well, if we're under water, they can't fight us, and we can't fight them,' asserted Dorothy.

'They could kill the fishes, however,' said Ozma gravely.

'We have ways to fight, also, even though our island is under water,' claimed Lady Aurex. 'I cannot tell you all our secrets, but this island is full of surprises. Also our Queen's magic is astonishing.'

'Did she steal it all from the three Adepts in Sorcery that are now fishes?'

'She stole the knowledge and the magic tools, but she has used them as the three Adepts never would have done.'

By this time the top of the dome was quite under water and suddenly the island stopped sinking and became stationary.

'See!' cried Lady Aurex, pointing to the shore. 'The Flatheads have come.'

On the bank, which was now far above their heads, a crowd of dark figures could be seen.

'Now let us see what Coo-ee-oh will do to oppose them,' continued Lady Aurex, in a voice that betrayed her excitement.

The Flatheads, pushing their way through the line of palm trees, had reached the shore of the lake just as the top of the island's dome disappeared beneath the surface. The water now flowed from shore to shore, but through the clear water the dome was still visible and the houses of the Skeezers could be dimly seen through the panes of glass.

'Good!' exclaimed the Su-dic, who had armed all his followers and had brought with him two copper vessels, which he carefully set down upon the ground beside him. 'If Coo-ee-oh wants to hide instead of fighting our job will be easy, for in one of these copper vessels I have enough poison to kill every fish in the lake.'

'Kill them, then, while we have time, and then we can go home again,' advised one of the chief officers.

'Not yet,' objected the Su-dic. 'The Queen of the Skeezers has defied me, and I want to get her into my power, as well as to destroy her magic. She transformed my poor wife into a Golden Pig, and I must have revenge for that, whatever else we do.'

'Look out!' suddenly exclaimed the officers, pointing into the lake; 'something's going to happen.'

From the submerged dome a door opened and something black shot swiftly out into the water. The door instantly closed behind it and the dark object cleaved its way through the water, without rising to the surface, directly toward the place where the Flatheads were standing.

'What is that?' Dorothy asked the Lady Aurex.

'That is one of the Queen's submarines,' was the reply. 'It is all enclosed, and can move under water. Coo-ee-oh has several of these boats which are kept in little rooms in the basement under our village. When the island is submerged, the Queen uses these boats to reach the shore, and I believe she now intends to fight the Flatheads with them.'

The Su-dic and his people knew nothing of Coo-ee-oh's submarines, so they watched with surprise as the under-water boat approached them. When it was quite near the

shore it rose to the surface and the top parted and fell back, disclosing a boat full of armed Skeezers. At the head was the Queen, standing up in the bow and holding in one hand a coil of magic rope that gleamed like silver.

The boat halted and Coo-ee-oh drew back her arm to throw the silver rope toward the Su-dic, who was now but a few feet from her. But the wily Flathead leader quickly realized his danger and before the Queen could throw the rope he caught up one of the copper vessels and dashed its contents full in her face!

11

The Conquest of the Skeezers

QUEEN COO-EE-OH dropped the rope, tottered and fell headlong into the water, sinking beneath the surface, while the Skeezers in the submarine were too bewildered to assist her and only stared at the ripples in the water where she had disappeared. A moment later there arose to the surface a beautiful White Swan. This Swan was of large size, very gracefully formed, and scattered all over its white feathers were tiny diamonds, so thickly placed that as the rays of the morning sun fell upon them the entire body of the Swan glistened like one brilliant diamond. The head of the Diamond Swan had a bill of polished gold and its eyes were two sparkling amethysts.

'Hooray!' cried the Su-dic, dancing up and down with wicked glee. 'My poor wife, Rora, is avenged at last. You made her a Golden Pig, Coo-ee-oh, and now I have made you a Diamond Swan. Float on your lake forever, if you like, for your web feet can do no more magic and you are as powerless as the Pig you made of my wife!'

'Villain! Scoundrel!' croaked the Diamond Swan. 'You will be punished for this. Oh, what a fool I was to let you enchant me!'

'A fool you were, and a fool you are!' laughed the Su-dic, dancing madly in his delight. And then he carelessly tipped over the other copper vessel with his heel and its contents spilled on the sands and were lost to the last drop.

The Su-dic stopped short and looked at the overturned vessel with a rueful countenance.

'That's too bad – too bad!' he exclaimed sorrowfully. 'I've lost all the poison I had to kill the fishes with, and I can't make any more because only my wife knew the secret of it, and she is now a foolish Pig and has forgotten all her magic.'

'Very well,' said the Diamond Swan scornfully, as she floated upon the water and swam gracefully here and there. 'I'm glad to see you are foiled. Your punishment is just beginning, for although you have enchanted me and taken away my powers of sorcery you have still the three magic fishes to deal with, and they'll destroy you in time, mark my words.'

The Su-dic stared at the Swan a moment. Then he yelled to his men:

'Shoot her! Shoot the saucy bird!'

They let fly some arrows at the Diamond Swan, but she dived under the water and the missiles fell harmlessly. When Coo-ee-oh rose to the surface she was far from the shore and she swiftly swam across the lake to where no arrows or spears could reach her.

The Su-dic rubbed his chin and thought what to do next. Near by floated the submarine in which the Queen had come, but the Skeezers who were in it were puzzled what to do with themselves. Perhaps they were not sorry their cruel mistress had been transformed into a Diamond Swan, but the transformation had left them quite helpless. The under-water boat was not operated by machinery, but by certain mystic words uttered by Coo-ee-oh. They didn't know how to submerge it, or how to make the water-tight shield cover them again, or how to make the boat go back to the castle, or make it enter the little basement room where it was usually kept. As a matter of fact, they were now shut out of their village under the Great Dome and could not get back again. So one of the men called to the Supreme Dictator of the Flatheads, saying:

'Please make us prisoners and take us to your mountain, and feed and keep us, for we have nowhere to go.'

Then the Su-dic laughed and answered:

'Not so. I can't be bothered by caring for a lot of stupid Skeezers. Stay where you are, or go wherever you please, so long as you keep away from our mountain.' He turned to his men and added: 'We have conquered Queen Coo-ee-oh and made her a helpless swan. The Skeezers are under water and may stay there. So, having won the war, let us go home again and make merry and feast, having after many years proved the Flatheads to be greater and more powerful than the Skeezers.'

So the Flatheads marched away and passed through the row of palms and went back to their mountain, where the Su-dic and a few of his officers feasted and all the others were forced to wait on them.

'I'm sorry we couldn't have roast pig,' said the Su-dic, 'but as the only pig we have is made of gold, we can't eat her. Also the Golden Pig happens to be my wife, and even were she not gold I am sure she would be too tough to eat.'

12

The Diamond Swan

WHEN the Flatheads had gone away the Diamond Swan swam back to the boat and one of the young Skeezers named Ervic said to her eagerly:

'How can we get back to the island, your Majesty?'

'Am I not beautiful?' asked Coo-ee-oh, arching her neck gracefully and spreading her diamond-sprinkled wings. 'I can see my reflection in the water, and I'm sure there is no bird nor beast, nor human as magnificent as I am!'

'How shall we get back to the island, your Majesty?' pleaded Ervic.

'When my fame spreads throughout the land, people will travel from all parts of this lake to look upon my loveliness,' said Coo-ee-oh, shaking her feathers to make the diamonds glitter more brilliantly.

'But, your Majesty, we must go home and we do not know how to get there,' Ervic persisted.

'My eyes,' remarked the Diamond Swan, 'are wonderfully blue and bright and will charm all beholders.'

'Tell us how to make the boat go – how to get back into the island,' begged Ervic and the others cried just as earnestly: 'Tell us, Coo-ee-oh; tell us!'

'I don't know,' replied the Queen in a careless tone.

'You are a magic-worker, a sorceress, a witch!'

'I was, of course, when I was a girl,' she said, bending her head over the clear water to catch her reflection in it; 'but now I've forgotten all such foolish things as magic. Swans are lovelier than girls, especially when they're

sprinkled with diamonds. Don't you think so?' And she gracefully swam away, without seeming to care whether they answered or not.

Ervic and his companions were in despair. They saw plainly that Coo-ee-oh could not or would not help them. The former Queen had no further thought for her island, her people, or her wonderful magic; she was only intent on admiring her own beauty.

'Truly,' said Ervic, in a gloomy voice, 'the Flatheads have conquered us!'

Some of these events had been witnessed by Ozma and Dorothy and Lady Aurex, who had left the house and gone close to the glass of the dome, in order to see what was going on. Many of the Skeezers had also crowded against the dome, wondering what would happen next. Although their vision was to an extent blurred by the water and the necessity of looking upward at an angle, they had observed the main points of the drama enacted above. They saw Queen Coo-ee-oh's submarine come to the surface and open; they saw the Queen standing erect to throw her magic rope; they saw her sudden transformation into a Diamond Swan, and a cry of amazement went up from the Skeezers inside the dome.

'Good!' exclaimed Dorothy. 'I hate that old Su-dic, but I'm glad Coo-ee-oh is punished.'

'This is a dreadful misfortune!' cried Lady Aurex, pressing her hands upon her heart.

'Yes,' agreed Ozma, nodding her head thoughtfully; 'Coo-ee-oh's misfortune will prove a terrible blow to her people.'

'What do you mean by that?' asked Dorothy in surprise. 'Seems to *me* the Skeezers are in luck to lose their cruel Queen.'

'If that were all you would be right,' responded Lady Aurex; 'and if the island were above water it would not be so serious. But here we all are, at the bottom of the lake, and fast prisoners in this dome.'

'Can't you raise the island?' inquired Dorothy.

'No. Only Coo-ee-oh knew how to do that,' was the answer.

'We can try,' insisted Dorothy. 'If it can be made to go down, it can be made to come up. The machinery is still here, I suppose.'

'Yes; but the machinery works by magic, and Coo-ee-oh would never share her secret power with any one of us.'

Dorothy's face grew grave; but she was thinking.

'Ozma knows a lot of magic,' she said.

'But not that kind of magic,' Ozma replied.

'Can't you learn how, by looking at the machinery?'

'I'm afraid not, my dear. It isn't fairy magic at all; it is witchcraft.'

'Well,' said Dorothy, turning to Lady Aurex, 'you say there are other sub-sub-sinking boats. We can get in one of those, and shoot out to the top of the water, like Coo-ee-oh did, and so escape. And then we can help to rescue all the Skeezers down here.'

'No one knows how to work the under-water boats but the Queen,' declared Lady Aurex.

'Isn't there any door or window in this dome that we could open?'

'No; and, if there were, the water would rush in to flood the dome, and we could not get out.'

'The Skeezers,' said Ozma, 'could not drown; they only get wet and soggy and in that condition they would be very uncomfortable and unhappy. But *you* are a mortal girl, Dorothy, and if your Magic Belt protected you from death you would have to lie for ever at the bottom of the lake.'

'No, I'd rather die quickly,' asserted the little girl. 'But there are doors in the basement that open – to let out the bridges and the boats – and that would not flood the dome, you know.'

'Those doors open by a magic word, and only Coo-ee-oh knows the word that must be uttered,' said Lady Aurex.

'Dear me!' exclaimed Dorothy, 'that dreadful Queen's witchcraft upsets all my plans to escape. I guess I'll give it up, Ozma, and let *you* save us.'

Ozma smiled, but her smile was not so cheerful as usual. The Princess of Oz found herself confronted with a serious problem, and although she had no thought of despairing she realized that the Skeezers and their island, as well as Dorothy and herself, were in grave trouble and that unless she could find a means to save them they would be lost to the Land of Oz for all future time.

'In such a dilemma,' said she, musingly, 'nothing is gained by haste. Careful thought may aid us, and so may the course of events. The unexpected is always likely to happen, and cheerful patience is better than reckless action.'

'All right,' returned Dorothy; 'take your time, Ozma; there's no hurry. How about some breakfast, Lady Aurex?'

Their hostess led them back to the house, where she ordered her trembling servants to prepare and serve breakfast. All the Skeezers were frightened and anxious over the transformation of their Queen into a swan. Coo-ee-oh was feared and hated, but they had depended on her magic to conquer the Flatheads and she was the only one who could raise their island to the surface of the lake again.

Before breakfast was over several of the leading Skeezers came to Aurex to ask her advice and to question Princess Ozma, of whom they knew nothing except that she claimed to be a fairy and the Ruler of all the land, including the Lake of the Skeezers.

'If what you told Queen Coo-ee-oh was the truth,' they said to her, 'you are our lawful mistress, and we may depend on you to get us out of our difficulties.'

'I will try to do that,' Ozma graciously assured them, 'but you must remember that the powers of fairies are granted them to bring comfort and happiness to all who appeal to them. On the contrary, such magic as Coo-ee-oh knew and practised is unlawful witchcraft and her arts are such as no fairy would condescend to use. However, it is sometimes necessary to consider evil in order to accomplish good, and perhaps by studying Coo-ee-oh's tools and charms of witchcraft I may be able to save us. Do you promise to accept me as your Ruler and to obey my commands?'

They promised willingly.

'Then,' continued Ozma, 'I will go to Coo-ee-oh's palace and take possession of it. Perhaps what I find there will be of use to me. In the meantime tell all the Skeezers to fear nothing, but have patience. Let them return to their homes and perform their daily tasks as usual. Coo-ee-oh's loss may not prove a misfortune, but rather a blessing.'

This speech cheered the Skeezers amazingly. Really, they had no one now to depend upon but Ozma, and in spite of their dangerous position their hearts were lightened by the transformation and absence of their cruel Queen.

They got out their brass band and a grand procession escorted Ozma and Dorothy to the palace, where all of Coo-ee-oh's former servants were eager to wait upon them. Ozma invited Lady Aurex to stay at the palace also, for she knew all about the Skeezers and their island and had also been a favourite of the former Queen, so her advice and information were sure to prove valuable.

Ozma was somewhat disappointed in what she found in the palace. One room of Coo-ee-oh's private suite was entirely devoted to the practice of witchcraft, and here

were countless queer instruments and jars of ointments
and bottles of potions labelled with queer names, and
strange machines that Ozma could not guess the use of, and
pickled toads and snails and lizards, and a shelf of books
that were written in blood, but in a language which the
Ruler of Oz did not know.

'I do not see,' said Ozma to Dorothy, who accompanied
her in her search, 'how Coo-ee-oh knew the use of the magic
tools she stole from the three Adept Witches. Moreover, from
all reports these Adepts practised only good witchcraft,
such as would be helpful to their people, while Coo-ee-oh
performed only evil.'

'Perhaps she turned the good things to evil uses?' suggested Dorothy.

'Yes, and with the knowledge she gained Coo-ee-oh
doubtless invented many evil things quite unknown to the
good Adepts, who are now fishes,' added Ozma. 'It is un-
fortunate for us that the Queen kept her secrets so closely
guarded, for no one but herself could use any of these strange
things gathered in this room.'

'Couldn't we capture the Diamond Swan and make her
tell the secrets?' asked Dorothy.

'No; even were we able to capture her, Coo-ee-oh now
has forgotten all the magic she ever knew. But until we
ourselves escape from this dome we could not capture the
Swan, and were we to escape we would have no use for
Coo-ee-oh's magic.'

'That's a fact,' admitted Dorothy. 'But – say, Ozma, here's
a good idea! Couldn't we capture the three fishes – the gold
and silver and bronze ones, and couldn't you transform 'em
back to their own shapes, and then couldn't the three Adepts
get us out of here?'

'You are not very practical, Dorothy dear. It would be

as hard for us to capture the three fishes, from among all the other fishes in the lake, as to capture the Swan.'

'But if we could, it would be more help to us,' persisted the little girl.

'That is true,' answered Ozma, smiling at her friend's eagerness. 'You find a way to catch the fish, and I'll promise when they are caught to restore them to their proper forms.'

'I know you think I can't do it,' replied Dorothy, 'but I'm going to try.'

She left the palace and went to a place where she could look through a clear pane of the glass dome into the surrounding water. Immediately she became interested in the queer sights that met her view.

The Lake of the Skeezers was inhabited by fishes of many kinds and many sizes. The water was so transparent that the girl could see for a long distance and the fishes came so close to the glass of the dome that sometimes they actually touched it. On the white sands at the bottom of the lake were star-fish, lobsters, crabs and many shell fish of strange shapes and with shells of gorgeous hues. The water foliage was of brilliant colours and to Dorothy it resembled a splendid garden.

But the fishes were the most interesting of all. Some were big and lazy, floating slowly along or lying at rest with just their fins waving. Many with big round eyes looked full at the girl as she watched them and Dorothy wondered if they could hear her through the glass if she spoke to them. In Oz, where all the animals and birds can talk, many fishes are able to talk also, but usually they are more stupid than birds and animals because they think slowly and haven't much to talk about.

In the Lake of the Skeezers the fish of smaller size were more active than the big ones and darted quickly in and out among the swaying weeds, as if they had important business and were in a hurry. It was among the smaller varieties that Dorothy hoped to spy the gold and silver and bronze fishes. She had an idea the three would keep together, being companions now as they were in their natural forms, but such a multitude of fishes constantly passed, the scene shifting every moment, that she was not sure she would notice them even if they appeared in view. Her eyes couldn't look in all directions and the fishes she sought might be on the other side of the dome, or far away in the lake.

'P'raps, because they were afraid of Coo-ee-oh, they've hid themselves somewhere, and don't know their enemy has been transformed,' she reflected.

She watched the fishes for a long time, until she became hungry and went back to the palace for lunch. But she was not discouraged.

'Anything new, Ozma?' she asked.

'No, dear. Did you discover the three fishes?'

'Not yet. But there isn't anything better for me to do, Ozma, so I guess I'll go back and watch again.'

13

The Alarm Bell

GLINDA, THE GOOD, in her palace in the Quadling Country, had many things to occupy her mind, for not only did she look after the weaving and embroidery of her bevy of maids, and assist all those who came to her to implore her help – beasts and birds as well as people – but she was a close student of the arts of sorcery and spent much time in her Magical Laboratory, where she strove to find a remedy for every evil and to perfect her skill in magic.

Nevertheless, she did not forget to look in the Great Book of Records each day to see if any mention was made of the visit of Ozma and Dorothy to the Enchanted Mountain of the Flatheads and the Magic Isle of the Skeezers. The Records told her that Ozma had arrived at the mountain, that she had escaped, with her companion, and gone to the island of the Skeezers, and that Queen Coo-ee-oh had submerged the island so that it was entirely under water. Then came the statement that the Flatheads had come to the lake to poison the fishes and that their Supreme Dictator had transformed Queen Coo-ee-oh into a swan.

No other details were given in the Great Book and so Glinda did not know that since Coo-ee-oh had forgotten her magic none of the Skeezers knew how to raise the island to the surface again. So Glinda was not worried about Ozma and Dorothy until one morning, while she sat with her maids, there came a sudden clang of the great alarm bell. This was so unusual that every maid gave a start and even the Sorceress for a moment could not think what the alarm meant.

Then she remembered the ring she had given Dorothy when she left the palace to start on her venture. In giving the ring Glinda had warned the little girl not to use its magic powers unless she and Ozma were in real danger, but then she was to turn it on her finger once to the right and once to the left and Glinda's alarm bell would ring.

So the Sorceress now knew that danger threatened her beloved Ruler and Princess Dorothy, and she hurried to her magic room to seek information as to what sort of danger it was. The answer to her question was not very satisfactory, for it was only: 'Ozma and Dorothy are prisoners in the great Dome of the Isle of the Skeezers, and the Dome is under the water of the lake.'

'Hasn't Ozma the power to raise the island to the surface?' inquired Glinda.

'No,' was the reply, and the Record refused to say more except that Queen Coo-ee-oh, who alone could command the island to rise, had been transformed by the Flathead Su-dic into a Diamond Swan.

Then Glinda consulted the past records of the Skeezers in the Great Book. After diligent search she discovered that Coo-ee-oh was a powerful sorceress, who had gained most of her power by treacherously transforming the Adepts of Magic, who were visiting her, into three fishes – gold, silver and bronze – after which she had them cast into the lake.

Glinda reflected earnestly on this information and decided that someone must go to Ozma's assistance. While there was no great need of haste, because Ozma and Dorothy could live in a submerged dome a long time, it was evident they could not get out until someone was able to raise the island.

The Sorceress looked through all her recipes and books of sorcery, but could find no magic that would raise a sunken island. Such a thing had never before been required in sorcery. Then Glinda made a little island, covered by a glass dome, and sunk it in a pond near her castle, and experimented in magical ways to bring it to the surface. She made several such experiments, but all were failures. It seemed a simple thing to do, yet she could not do it.

Nevertheless, the wise Sorceress did not despair of finding a way to liberate her friends. Finally she concluded that the best thing to do was to go to the Skeezer country and examine the lake. While there she was more likely to discover a solution to the problem that bothered her, and to work out a plan for the rescue of Ozma and Dorothy.

So Glinda summoned her storks and her aerial chariot, and telling her maids she was going on a journey and might not soon return, she entered the chariot and was carried swiftly to the Emerald City.

In Princess Ozma's place the Scarecrow was now acting as Ruler of the Land of Oz. There wasn't much for him to do, because all the affairs of state moved so smoothly, but he was there in case anything unforeseen should happen.

Glinda found the Scarecrow playing croquet with Trot and Betsy Bobbin, two little girls who lived at the palace under Ozma's protection and were great friends of Dorothy and much loved by all the Oz people.

'Something's happened!' cried Trot, as the chariot of the Sorceress descended near them. 'Glinda never comes here 'cept something's gone wrong.'

'I hope no harm has come to Ozma, or Dorothy,' said Betsy anxiously, as the lovely Sorceress stepped down from her chariot.

Glinda approached the Scarecrow and told him of the dilemma of Ozma and Dorothy and she added: 'We must save them, somehow, Scarecrow.'

'Of course,' replied the Scarecrow, stumbling over a hoop and falling flat on his painted face.

The girls picked him up and patted his straw stuffing into shape, and he continued, as if nothing had occurred: 'But you'll have to tell me what to do, for I never have raised a sunken island in all my life.'

'We must have a Council of State as soon as possible,' proposed the Sorceress. 'Please send messengers to summon all of Ozma's counsellors to this palace. Then we can decide what is best to be done.'

The Scarecrow lost no time in doing this. Fortunately most of the royal counsellors were in the Emerald City or near to it, so they all met in the throne room of the palace that same evening.

14

Ozma's Counsellors

No Ruler ever had such a queer assortment of advisers as the Princess Ozma had gathered about her throne. Indeed, in no other country could such amazing people exist. But Ozma loved them for their peculiarities and could trust every one of them.

First there was the Tin Woodman. Every bit of him was tin, brightly polished. All his joints were kept well oiled and moved smoothly. He carried a gleaming axe to prove he was a woodman, but seldom had cause to use it because he lived in a magnificent tin castle in the Winkie Country of Oz and was the Emperor of all the Winkies. The Tin Woodman's name was Nick Chopper. He had a very good mind, but his heart was not of much account, so he was very careful to do nothing unkind or to hurt anyone's feelings.

Another counsellor was Scraps, the Patchwork Girl of Oz, who was made of a gaudy patchwork quilt, cut into shape and stuffed with cotton. This Patchwork Girl was very intelligent, but so full of fun and mad pranks that a lot of more stupid folks thought she must be crazy. Scraps was jolly under all conditions, however grave they might be, but her laughter and good spirits were of value in cheering others and in her seemingly careless remarks much wisdom could often be found.

Then there was the Shaggy Man – shaggy from head to foot, hair and whiskers, clothes and shoes – but very kind and gentle and one of Ozma's most loyal supporters.

Tik-Tok was there, a copper man with machinery inside

him, so cleverly constructed that he moved, spoke and thought by three separate clock-works. Tik-Tok was very reliable because he always did exactly what he was wound up to do, but his machinery was liable to run down at times and then he was quite helpless until wound up again.

A different sort of person was Jack Pumpkinhead, one of Ozma's oldest friends and her companion on many adventures. Jack's body was very crude and awkward, being formed of limbs of trees of different sizes, jointed with wooden pegs. But it was a substantial body and not likely to break or wear out, and when it was dressed the clothes covered much of its roughness. The head of Jack Pumpkinhead was, as you have guessed, a ripe pumpkin, with the eyes, nose and mouth carved upon one side. The pumpkin was stuck on Jack's wooden neck and was liable to get turned sideways or backward and then he would have to straighten it with his wooden hands.

The worst thing about this sort of a head was that it did not keep well and was sure to spoil sooner or later. So Jack's main business was to grow a field of fine pumpkins each year, and always before his old head spoiled he would select a fresh pumpkin from the field and carve the features on it very neatly, and have it ready to replace the old head whenever it became necessary. He didn't always carve it the same way, so his friends never knew exactly what sort of an expression they would find on his face. But there was no mistaking him, because he was the only pumpkin-headed man alive in the Land of Oz.

A one-legged sailor-man was a member of Ozma's council. His name was Cap'n Bill and he had come to the Land of Oz with Trot, and had been made welcome on account of his cleverness, honesty and good-nature. He wore a wooden leg to replace the one he had lost and was a great friend of all the children in Oz because he could whittle all sorts of toys out of wood with his big jack-knife.

Professor H. M. Wogglebug, T. E., was another member of the council. The 'H. M.' meant Highly Magnified, for the Professor was once a little bug, who became magnified to the size of a man and always remained so. The 'T.E.' meant that he was Thoroughly Educated. He was at the head of Princess Ozma's Royal Athletic College, and so that the students would not have to study and so lose much time that could be devoted to athletic sports, such as football, baseball and the like, Professor Wogglebug had invented the famous Educational Pills. If one of the college students took a Geography Pill after breakfast, he knew his geography lesson in an instant; if he took a Spelling Pill he at once knew his spelling lesson, and an Arithmetic Pill enabled the student to do any kind of sum without having to think about it.

These useful pills made the college very popular and taught the boys and girls of Oz their lessons in the easiest possible way. In spite of this, Professor Wogglebug was not a favourite outside his college, for he was very conceited and admired himself so much and displayed his cleverness and learning so constantly, that no one cared to associate with him. Ozma found him of value in her councils, nevertheless.

Perhaps the most splendidly dressed of all those present was a great frog as large as a man, called the Frogman, who was noted for his wise sayings. He had come to the Emerald City from the Yip Country of Oz and was a guest of honour. His long-tailed coat was of velvet, his vest of satin and his trousers of finest silk. There were diamond buckles on his shoes and he carried a gold-headed cane and a high silk hat. All of the bright colours were represented in his rich attire, so it tired one's eyes to look at him for long, until one became used to his splendour.

The best farmer in all Oz was Uncle Henry, who was Dorothy's own uncle, and who now lived near the Emerald City with his wife Aunt Em. Uncle Henry taught the Oz people how to grow the finest vegetables and fruits and grains and was of much use to Ozma in keeping the Royal Storehouses well filled. He, too, was a counsellor.

The reason I mention the little Wizard of Oz last is because he was the most important man in the Land of Oz. He wasn't a big man in size, but he was a big man in power and intelligence and second only to Glinda the Good in all the mystic arts of magic. Glinda had taught him, and the Wizard and the Sorceress were the only ones in Oz permitted by law to practise wizardry and sorcery, which they applied only to good uses and for the benefit of the people.

The Wizard wasn't exactly handsome but he was pleasant to look at. His bald head was as shiny as if it had been varnished; there was always a merry twinkle in his eyes and he was as spry as a schoolboy. Dorothy says the reason the Wizard is not as powerful as Glinda is because Glinda didn't teach him all she knows, but what the Wizard knows he knows very well and so he performs some very remarkable magic.

The ten I have mentioned assembled, with the Scarecrow and Glinda, in Ozma's throne room, right after dinner that evening, and the Sorceress told them all she knew of the plight of Ozma and Dorothy.

'Of course we must rescue them,' she continued, 'and the sooner they are rescued the better pleased they will be; but what we must now determine is how they can be saved. That is why I have called you together in council.'

'The easiest way,' remarked the Shaggy Man, 'is to raise the sunken island of the Skeezers to the top of the water again.'

'Tell me how?' said Glinda.

'I don't know how, your Highness, for I have never raised a sunken island.'

'We might all get under it and lift,' suggested Professor Wogglebug.

'How can we get under it when it rests on the bottom of the lake?' asked the Sorceress.

'Couldn't we throw a rope around it and pull it ashore?' inquired Jack Pumpkinhead.

'Why not pump the water out of the lake?' suggested the Patchwork Girl with a laugh.

'Do be sensible!' pleaded Glinda. 'This is a serious matter, and we must give it serious thought.'

'How big is the lake and how big is the island?' was the Frogman's question.

'None of us can tell, for we have not been there.'

'In that case,' said the Scarecrow, 'it appears to me we ought to go to the Skeezer country and examine it carefully.'

'Quite right,' agreed the Tin Woodman.

'We-will-have-to-go-there-any-how,' remarked Tik-Tok in his jerky machine voice.

'The question is which of us shall go, and how many of us?' said the Wizard.

'I shall go of course,' declared the Scarecrow.

'And I,' said Scraps.

'It is my duty to Ozma to go,' asserted the Tin Woodman.

'I could not stay away, knowing our loved Princess is in danger,' said the Wizard.

'We all feel like that,' Uncle Henry said.

Finally one and all present decided to go to the Skeezer country, with Glinda and the little Wizard to lead them. Magic must meet magic in order to conquer it, so these two skilful magic-workers were necessary to insure the success of the expedition.

They were all ready to start at a moment's notice, for

none had any affairs of importance to attend to. Jack was wearing a newly made Pumpkin-head and the Scarecrow had recently been stuffed with fresh straw. Tik-Tok's machinery was in good running order and the Tin Woodman always was well oiled.

'It is quite a long journey,' said Glinda, 'and while I might travel quickly to the Skeezer country by means of my stork chariot the rest of you will be obliged to walk. So, as we must keep together, I will send my chariot back to my castle and we will plan to leave the Emerald City at sunrise tomorrow.'

15

The Great Sorceress

BETSY and Trot, when they heard of the rescue expedition, begged the Wizard to permit them to join it and he consented. The Glass Cat, overhearing the conversation, wanted to go also and to this the Wizard made no objection.

This Glass Cat was one of the real curiosities of Oz. It had been made and brought to life by a clever magician named Dr Pipt, who was not now permitted to work magic and was an ordinary citizen of the Emerald City. The cat was of transparent glass, through which one could plainly see its ruby heart beating and its pink brains whirling around in the top of the head.

The Glass Cat's eyes were emeralds; its fluffy tail was of spun glass and very beautiful. The ruby heart, while pretty to look at, was hard and cold and the Glass Cat's disposition was not pleasant at all times. It scorned to catch mice, did not eat, and was extremely lazy. If you complimented the remarkable cat on her beauty, she would be very friendly, for she loved admiration above everything. The pink brains were always working and their owner was indeed more intelligent than most common cats.

Three other additions to the rescue party were made the next morning, just as they were setting out upon their journey. The first was a little boy called Button Bright, because he had no other name that anyone could remember. He was a fine, manly little fellow, well mannered and good humoured, who had only one bad fault. He was continually getting lost. To be sure, Button Bright got found

as often as he got lost, but when he was missing his friends
could not help being anxious about him.

'Some day,' predicted the Patchwork Girl, 'he won't be
found, and that will be the last of him.' But that didn't
worry Button Bright, who was so careless that he did not
seem to be able to break the habit of getting lost.

The second addition to the party was a Munchkin boy

of about Button Bright's age, named Ojo. He was often called 'Ojo the Lucky', because good fortune followed him wherever he went. He and Button Bright were close friends, although of such different natures, and Trot and Betsy were fond of both.

The third and last to join the expedition was an enormous lion, one of Ozma's regular guardians and the most important and intelligent beast in all Oz. He called himself the Cowardly Lion, saying that every little danger scared him so badly that his heart thumped against his ribs, but all who knew him knew that the Cowardly Lion's fears were coupled with bravery and that however much he might be frightened he summoned courage to meet every danger he encountered. Often he had saved Dorothy and Ozma in times of peril, but afterward he moaned and trembled and wept because he had been so scared.

'If Ozma needs help, I'm going to help her,' said the great beast. 'Also, I suspect the rest of you may need me on the journey – especially Trot and Betsy – for you may pass through a dangerous part of the country. I know that wild Gillikin country pretty well. Its forests harbour many ferocious beasts.'

They were glad the Cowardly Lion was to join them, and in good spirits the entire party formed a procession and marched out of the Emerald City amid the shouts of the people, who wished them success and a safe return with their beloved Ruler.

They followed a different route from that taken by Ozma and Dorothy, for they went through the Winkie Country and up north toward Oogaboo. But before they got there they swerved to the left and entered the Great Gillikin Forest, the nearest thing to a wilderness in all Oz. Even the Cowardly Lion had to admit that certain parts of this forest were unknown to him, although he had often wandered among the trees, and the Scarecrow and Tin Woodman, who were great travellers, never had been there at all.

The forest was only reached after a tedious tramp, for some of the Rescue Expedition were quite awkward on their feet. The Patchwork Girl was as light as a feather and very spry; the Tin Woodman covered the ground as easily as Uncle Henry and the Wizard; but Tik-Tok moved slowly and the slightest obstruction in the road would halt him until the others cleared it away. Then, too, Tik-Tok's machinery kept running down, so Betsy and Trot took turns in winding it up.

The Scarecrow was more clumsy but less bother, for although he often stumbled and fell he could scramble up again and a little patting of his straw-stuffed body would put him in good shape again.

Another awkward one was Jack Pumpkinhead, for walking would jar his head around on his neck and then he would be likely to go in the wrong direction. But the Frogman took Jack's arm and then he followed the path more easily.

Cap'n Bill's wooden leg didn't prevent him from keeping up with the others and the old sailor could walk as far as any of them.

When they entered the forest the Cowardly Lion took the lead. There was no path here for men, but many beasts had made paths of their own which only the eyes of the Lion, practised in woodcraft, could discern. So he stalked ahead and wound his way in and out, the others following in single file, Glinda being next to the Lion.

There are dangers in the forest, of course, but as the huge Lion headed the party he kept the wild denizens of the wilderness from bothering the travellers. Once, to be sure, an enormous leopard sprang upon the Glass Cat and caught her in his powerful jaws, but he broke several of his teeth

and with howls of pain and dismay dropped his prey and vanished among the trees.

'Are you hurt?' Trot anxiously inquired of the Glass Cat. 'How silly!' exclaimed the creature in an irritated tone of voice; 'nothing can hurt glass, and I'm too solid to break easily. But I'm annoyed at that leopard's impudence. He has no respect for beauty or intelligence. If he had noticed my pink brains work, I'm sure he would have realized I'm too important to be grabbed in a wild beast's jaws.'

'Never mind,' said Trot consolingly; 'I'm sure he won't do it again.'

They were almost in the centre of the forest when Ojo, the Munchkin boy, suddenly said: 'Why, where's Button Bright?'

They halted and looked around them. Button Bright was not with the party.

'Dear me,' remarked Betsy, 'I expect he's lost again!'

'When did you see him last, Ojo?' inquired Glinda.

'It was some time ago,' replied Ojo. 'He was trailing along at the end and throwing twigs at the squirrels in the trees. Then I went to talk to Betsy and Trot, and just now I noticed he was gone.'

'This is too bad,' declared the Wizard, 'for it is sure to delay our journey. We must find Button Bright before we go any farther, for this forest is full of ferocious beasts that would not hesitate to tear the boy to pieces.'

'But what shall we do?' asked the Scarecrow. 'If any of us leaves the party to search for Button Bright he or she might fall a victim to the beasts, and if the Lion leaves us we will have no protector.

'The Glass Cat could go,' suggested the Frogman. 'The beasts can do her no harm, as we have discovered.'

The Wizard turned to Glinda.

'Cannot your sorcery discover where Button Bright is?' he asked.

'I think so,' replied the Sorceress.

She called to Uncle Henry, who had been carrying her wicker box, to bring it to her, and when he obeyed she opened it and drew out a small round mirror. On the surface of the glass she dusted a white powder and then wiped it away with her handkerchief and looked in the mirror. It reflected a part of the forest, and there, beneath a wide-spreading tree, Button Bright was lying asleep. On one side of him crouched a tiger, ready to spring; on the other side was a big grey wolf, its bared fangs glistening in a wicked way.

'Goodness me!' cried Trot, looking over Glinda's shoulder. 'They'll catch and kill him sure.'

Everyone crowded around for a glimpse at the magic mirror.

'Pretty bad – pretty bad!' said the Scarecrow sorrowfully.

'Comes of getting lost!' said Cap'n Bill, sighing.

'Guess he's a goner!' said the Frogman, wiping his eyes on his purple silk handkerchief.

'But where is he?' Can't we save him?' asked Ojo the Lucky.

'If we knew where he is we could probably save him,' replied the little Wizard, 'but that tree looks so much like all the other trees, that we can't tell whether it's far away or near by.'

'Look at Glinda!' exclaimed Betsy.

Glinda, having handed the mirror to the Wizard, had stepped aside and was making strange passes with her outstretched arms and reciting in low, sweet tones a mystical incantation. Most of them watched the Sorceress with anxious eyes, despair giving way to the hope that she might be able to save their friend. The Wizard, however, watched the scene in the mirror, while over his shoulders peered Trot, the Scarecrow and the Shaggy Man.

What they saw was more strange than Glinda's actions. The tiger started to spring on the sleeping boy, but suddenly lost its power to move and lay flat upon the ground. The grey wolf seemed unable to lift its feet from the ground. It pulled first at one leg and then at another, and finding itself strangely confined to the spot began to back and snarl angrily. They couldn't hear the barkings and snarls, but they could see the creature's mouth open and its thick lips move. Button Bright, however, being but a few feet away from the wolf, heard its cries of rage, which wakened him from his untroubled sleep.

The boy sat up and looked first at the tiger and then at the wolf. His face showed that for a moment he was quite frightened, but he soon saw that the beasts were unable to approach him and so he got upon his feet and examined them curiously, with a mischievous smile upon his face. Then he deliberately kicked the tiger's head with his foot and catching up a fallen branch of a tree he went to the wolf and gave it a good whacking. Both the beasts were furious at such treatment but could not resent it.

Button Bright now threw down the stick and with his hands in his pockets wandered carelessly away.

'Now,' said Glinda, 'let the Glass Cat run and find him. He is in that direction,' pointing the way, 'but how far off I do not know. Make haste and lead him back to us as quickly as you can.'

The Glass Cat did not obey everyone's orders, but she really feared the great Sorceress, so as soon as the words were spoken the crystal animal darted away and was quickly lost to sight.

The Wizard handed the mirror back to Glinda, for the woodland scene had now faded from the glass. Then those who cared to rest sat down to await Button Bright's coming. It was not long before he appeared through the trees and as he rejoined his friends he said in a peevish tone:

'Don't ever send that Glass Cat to find me again. She was very impolite and, if we didn't all know that she had no manners, I'd say she insulted me.'

Glinda turned upon the boy sternly.

'You have caused all of us much anxiety and annoyance,' said she. 'Only my magic saved you from destruction. I forbid you to get lost again.'

'Of course,' he answered. 'It won't be *my* fault if I get lost again; but it wasn't my fault *this* time.'

16

The Enchanted Fishes

I MUST now tell you what happened to Ervic and the three other Skeezers who were left floating in the iron boat after Queen Coo-ee-oh had been transformed into a Diamond Swan by the magic of the Flathead Su-dic.

The four Skeezers were all young men and their leader was Ervic. Coo-ee-oh had taken them with her in the boat to assist her if she captured the Flat-headed chief, as she hoped to do by means of her silver rope. They knew nothing about the witchcraft that moved the submarine and so, when left floating upon the lake, were at a loss what to do. The submarine could not be submerged by them or made to return to the sunken island. There were neither oars nor sails in the boat, which was not anchored but drifted quietly upon the surface of the lake.

The Diamond Swan had no further thought or care for her people. She had sailed over to the other side of the lake and all the calls and pleadings of Ervic and his companions were unheeded by the vain bird. As there was nothing else for them to do, they sat quietly in their boat and waited as patiently as they could for someone to come to their aid.

The Flatheads had refused to help them and had gone back to their mountain. All the Skeezers were imprisoned in the Great Dome and could not help even themselves. When evening came, they saw the Diamond Swan, still keeping to the opposite shore of the lake, walk out of the water to the sands, shake her diamond-sprinkled feathers, and then disappear among the bushes to seek a resting place for the night.

'I'm hungry,' said Ervic.

'I'm cold,' said another Skeezer.

'I'm tired,' said a third.

'I'm afraid,' said the last one of them.

But it did them no good to complain. Night fell and the moon rose and cast a silvery sheen over the surface of the water.

'Go to sleep,' said Ervic to his companions. 'I'll stay awake and watch, for we may be rescued in some unexpected way.

So the other three laid themselves down in the bottom of the boat and were soon fast asleep.

Ervic watched. He rested himself by leaning over the bow of the boat, his face near to the moonlit water, and thought dreamily of the day's surprising events and wondered what would happen to the prisoners in the Great Dome.

Suddenly a tiny gold fish popped its head above the surface of the lake, not more than a foot from his eyes. A silver fish then raised its head beside that of the gold fish, and a moment later a bronze fish lifted its head beside the others. The three fish, all in a row, looked earnestly with their round, bright eyes into the astonished eyes of Ervic the Skeezer.

'We are the three Adepts whom Queen Coo-ee-oh betrayed and wickedly transformed,' said the gold fish, its voice low and soft but distinctly heard in the stillness of the night.

'I know of our Queen's treacherous deed,' replied Ervic, 'and I am sorry for your misfortune. Have you been in the lake ever since?'

'Yes,' was the reply.

'I – I hope you are well – and comfortable,' stammered Ervic, not knowing what else to say.

'We knew that some day Coo-ee-oh would meet with the fate she so richly deserves,' declared the bronze fish. 'We have waited and watched for this time. Now if you will promise to help us and will be faithful and true, you can aid us in regaining our natural forms, and save yourself and all your people from the dangers that now threaten you.'

'Well,' said Ervic, 'you can depend on my doing the best I can. But I'm no witch, nor magician, you must know.'

'All we ask is that you obey our instructions.' returned the silver fish. 'We know that you are honest and that you served Coo-ee-oh only because you were obliged to in order to escape her anger. Do as we command and all will be well.'

'I promise!' exclaimed the young man. 'Tell me what I am to do first.'

'You will find in the bottom of your boat the silver cord which dropped from Coo-ee-oh's hand when she was transformed,' said the gold fish. 'Tie one end of that cord to the bow of your boat and drop the other end to us in the water. together we will pull your boat to the shore.'

Ervic much doubted that the three small fishes could move so heavy a boat, but he did as he was told and the fishes all seized their end of the silver cord in their mouths and headed toward the nearest shore, which was the very place where the Flatheads had stood when they conquered Queen Coo-ee-oh.

At first the boat did not move at all, although the fishes pulled with all their strength. But presently the strain began to tell. Very slowly the boat crept toward the shore, gaining more speed at every moment. A couple of yards away from the sandy beach the fishes dropped the cord from their mouths and swam to one side, while the iron boat, being now under way, continued to move until its prow grated upon the sands.

Ervic leaned over the side and said to the fishes: 'What next?'

'You will find upon the sand,' said the silver fish, 'a copper kettle, which the Su-dic forgot when he went away. Cleanse it thoroughly in the water of the lake, for it has had poison in it. When it is cleaned, fill it with fresh water and hold it over the side of the boat, so that we three may swim into the kettle. We will then instruct you further.'

'Do you wish me to catch you, then?' asked Ervic in surprise.

'Yes,' was the reply.

So Ervic jumped out of the boat and found the copper kettle. Carrying it a little way down the beach, he washed it well, scrubbing away every drop of the poison it had contained with sand from the shore.

Then he went back to the boat.

Ervic's comrades were still sound asleep and knew nothing of the three fishes or what strange happenings were taking place about them. Ervic dipped the kettle in the lake, holding fast to the handle until it was under water. The gold and silver and bronze fishes promptly swam into the kettle. The young Skeezer then lifted it, poured out a little of the water so it would not spill over the edge, and said to the fishes: 'What next?'

'Carry the kettle to the shore. Take one hundred steps to the east, along the edge of the lake, and then you will see a path leading through the meadows, up hill and down dale. Follow the path until you come to a cottage which is painted a purple colour with white trimmings. When you stop at the gate of this cottage we will tell you what to do next. Be careful, above all, not to stumble and spill the water from the kettle, or you would destroy us and all you have done would be in vain.'

The gold fish issued these commands and Ervic promised to be careful and started to obey. He left his sleeping comrades in the boat, stepping cautiously over their bodies, and on reaching the shore took exactly one hundred steps to the east. Then he looked for the path and the moonlight was so bright that he easily discovered it, although it was hidden from view by tall weeds until one came full upon it. This path was very narrow and did not seem to be much used, but it was quite distinct and Ervic had no difficulty in following it. He walked through a broad meadow, covered with tall grass and weeds, up a hill and down into a valley and then up another hill and down again.

It seemed to Ervic that he had walked miles and miles. Indeed the moon sank low and day was beginning to dawn when finally he discovered by the roadside a pretty little cottage, painted purple with white trimmings. It was a lonely place – no other buildings were anywhere about and the ground was not tilled at all. No farmer lived here, that was certain. Who would care to dwell in such an isolated place?

But Ervic did not bother his head long with such questions. He went up to the gate that led to the cottage, set the copper kettle carefully down and bending over it asked:

'What next?'

Under the Great Dome

WHEN Glinda the Good and her followers of the Rescue Expedition came in sight of the Enchanted Mountain of the Flatheads, it was away to the left of them, for the route they had taken through the Great Forest was some distance from that followed by Ozma and Dorothy.

They halted awhile to decide whether they should call upon the Supreme Dictator first, or go on to the Lake of the Skeezers.

'If we go to the mountain,' said the Wizard, 'we may get into trouble with that wicked Su-dic, and then we would be delayed in rescuing Ozma and Dorothy. So I think our best plan will be to go to the Skeezer Country, raise the sunken island and save our friends and the imprisoned Skeezers. Afterward we can visit the mountain and punish the cruel magician of the Flatheads.'

'That is sensible,' approved the Shaggy Man. 'I quite agree with you.'

The others, too, seemed to think the Wizard's plan the best, and Glinda herself commended it, so on they marched toward the line of palm trees that hid the Skeezers' lake from view.

Pretty soon they came to the palms. These were set closely together, the branches, which came quite to the ground, being so tightly interlaced that even the Glass Cat could scarcely find a place to squeeze through. The path which the Flatheads used was some distance away.

'Here's a job for the Tin Woodman,' said the Scarecrow.

So the Tin Woodman, who was always glad to be of use, set to work with his sharp, gleaming axe, which he always carried, and in a surprisingly short time had chopped away enough branches to permit them all to pass easily through the trees.

Now the clear waters of the beautiful lake were before them and by looking closely they could see the outlines of the Great Dome of the sunken island, far from shore and directly in the centre of the lake.

Of course every eye was at first fixed upon this dome, where Ozma and Dorothy and the Skeezers were still fast prisoners. But soon their attention was caught by a more brilliant sight, for here was the Diamond Swan swimming just before them, its long neck arched proudly, the amethyst eyes gleaming and all the diamond-sprinkled feathers glistening splendidly under the rays of the sun.

'That,' said Glinda, 'is the transformation of Queen Coo-ee-oh, the haughty and wicked witch who betrayed the three Adepts at Magic and treated her people like slaves.'

'She's wonderfully beautiful now,' remarked the Frogman.

'It doesn't seem like much of a punishment,' said Trot. 'The Flathead Su-dic ought to have made her a toad.'

'I am sure Coo-ee-oh is punished,' said Glinda, 'for she has lost all her magic power and her grand palace and can no longer misrule the poor Skeezers.'

'Let us call to her, and hear what she has to say,' proposed the Wizard.

So Glinda beckoned the Diamond Swan, which swam gracefully to a position near them. Before anyone could speak Coo-ee-oh called to them in a rasping voice – for the voice of a swan is always harsh and unpleasant – and said with much pride:

'Admire me, Strangers! Admire the lovely Coo-ee-oh, the handsomest creature in all Oz. Admire me!'

'Handsome is as handsome does,' replied the Scarecrow. 'Are your deeds lovely, Coo-ee-oh?'

'Deeds? What deeds can a swan do but swim around and give pleasure to all beholders?' said the sparkling bird.

'Have you forgotten your former life? Have you forgotten your magic and witchcraft?' inquired the Wizard.

'Magic – witchcraft? Pshaw, who cares for such silly things?' retorted Coo-ee-oh. 'As for my past life, it seems like an unpleasant dream. I wouldn't go back to it if I could. Don't you admire my beauty, Strangers?'

'Tell us, Coo-ee-oh,' said Glinda earnestly, 'if you can recall enough of your witchcraft to enable us to raise the sunken island to the surface of the lake. Tell us that and I'll give you a string of pearls to wear around your neck and add to your beauty.'

'Nothing can add to my beauty, for I'm the most beautiful creature anywhere in the whole world.'

'But how can we raise the island?'

'I don't know and I don't care. If ever I knew I've forgotten, and I'm glad of it,' was the response. 'Just watch me circle around and see me glitter!'

'It's no use,' said Button Bright; 'the old Swan is too much in love with herself to think of anything else.'

'That's a fact,' agreed Betsy with a sigh; 'but we've got to get Ozma and Dorothy out of that lake, somehow or other.'

'And we must do it in our own way,' added the Scarecrow.

'But how?' asked Uncle Henry in a grave voice, for he could not bear to think of his dear niece Dorothy being out there under water; 'how shall we do it?'

'Leave that to Glinda,' advised the Wizard, realizing he was helpless to do it himself.

'If it were just an ordinary sunken island,' said the

powerful Sorceress, 'there would be several ways by which I might bring it to the surface again. But this is a Magic Isle, and by some curious art of witchcraft, unknown to any but Queen Coo-ee-oh, it obeys certain commands of magic and will not respond to any other. I do not despair in the least, but it will require some deep study to solve this difficult problem. If the Swan could only remember the witchcraft that she invented and knew as a woman, I could force her to tell me the secret, but all her former knowledge is now forgotten.'

'It seems to me,' said the Wizard after a brief silence had followed Glinda's speech, 'that there are three fishes in this lake that used to be Adepts at Magic and from whom Coo-ee-oh stole much of her knowledge. If we could find those fishes and return them to their former shapes, they could doubtless tell us what to do to bring the sunken island to the surface.'

'I have thought of those fishes,' replied Glinda, 'but among so many fishes as this lake contains how are we to single them out?'

You will understand, of course, that had Glinda been at home in her castle, where the Great Book of Records was, she would have known that Ervic the Skeezer already had taken the gold and silver and bronze fishes from the lake. But that act had been recorded in the Book after Glinda had set out on this journey, so it was all unknown to her.

'I think I see a boat yonder on the shore,' said Ojo the Munchkin boy, pointing to a place around the edge of the lake. 'If we could get that boat and row all over the lake, calling to the magic fishes, we might be able to find them.'

'Let us go to the boat,' said the Wizard.

They walked around the lake to where the boat was stranded upon the beach, but found it empty. It was a mere shell of blackened steel, with a collapsible roof that, when in position, made the submarine watertight, but at present the roof rested in slots on either side of the magic craft. There were no oars or sails, no machinery to make the boat go, and although Glinda promptly realized it was meant to be operated by witchcraft, she was not acquainted with that sort of magic.

'However,' said she, 'the boat is merely a boat, and I believe I can make it obey a command of sorcery, as well as it did the command of witchcraft. After I have given a little thought to the matter, the boat will take us wherever we desire to go.'

'Not all of us,' returned the Wizard, 'for it won't hold so many. But, most noble Sorceress, provided you can make the boat go, of what use will it be to us?'

'Can't we use it to catch the three fishes?' asked Button Bright.

'It will not be necessary to use the boat for that purpose,' replied Glinda. 'Wherever in the lake the enchanted fishes may be, they will answer to my call. What I am trying to discover is how the boat came to be on this shore, while the island on which it belongs is under water yonder. Did Coo-ee-oh come here in the boat to meet the Flatheads before the island was sunk, or afterwards?'

No one could answer that question, of course; but while they pondered the matter three young men advanced from the line of trees, and rather timidly bowed to the strangers.

'Who are you, and where did you come from?' inquired the Wizard.

'We are Skeezers,' answered one of them, 'and our home is on the Magic Isle of the Lake. We ran away when we saw you coming, and hid behind the trees, but as you are Strangers and seem to be friendly we decided to meet you, for we are in great trouble and need assistance.'

'If you belong on the island, why are you here?' demanded Glinda.

So they told her all the story: How the Queen had defied the Flatheads and submerged the whole island so that her enemies could not get to it or destroy it; how, when the Flatheads came to the shore, Coo-ee-oh had commanded them, together with their friend Ervic, to go with her in the submarine to conquer the Su-dic, and how the boat had shot out from the basement of the sunken isle, obeying a magic word, and risen to the surface, where it opened and floated upon the water.

Then followed the account of how the Su-dic had transformed Coo-ee-oh into a swan, after which she had forgotten all the witchcraft she ever knew. The young men told how, in the night when they were asleep, their comrade Ervic had mysteriously disappeared, while the boat in some strange manner had floated to the shore and stranded upon the beach.

That was all they knew. They had searched in vain for three days for Ervic. As their island was under water and they could not get back to it, the three Skeezers had no place to go, and so had waited patiently beside their boat for something to happen.

Being questioned by Glinda and the Wizard, they told all they knew about Ozma and Dorothy and declared the two girls were still in the village under the Great Dome. They were quite safe and would be well cared for by Lady Aurex, now that the Queen who opposed them was out of the way.

When they had gleaned all the information they could from these Skeezers, the Wizard said to Glinda:

'If you find you can make this boat obey your sorcery, you could have it return to the island, submerge itself, and enter the door in the basement from which it came. But I cannot see that our going to the sunken island would enable our friends to escape. We would only join them as prisoners.'

'Not so, friend Wizard,' replied Glinda. 'If the boat would obey my commands to enter the basement door, it would also obey my commands to come out again, and I could bring Ozma and Dorothy back with me.'

'And leave all of our people still imprisoned?' asked one of the Skeezers reproachfully.

'By making several trips in the boat, Glinda could fetch all your people to the shore,' replied the Wizard.

'But what could they do then?' inquired another Skeezer. 'They would have no homes and no place to go, and would be at the mercy of their enemies, the Flatheads.'

'That is true,' said Glinda the Good. 'And as these people are Ozma's subjects, I think she would refuse to escape with Dorothy and leave the others behind, or to abandon the island which is the lawful home of the Skeezers. I believe the best plan will be to summon the three fishes and learn from them how to raise the island.'

The little Wizard seemed to think that this was rather a forlorn hope.

'How will you summon them,' he asked the lovely Sorceress, 'and how can they hear you?'

'That is something we must consider carefully,' responded stately Glinda, with a serene smile. 'I think I can find a way.'

All of Ozma's counsellors applauded this sentiment, for they knew well the powers of the Sorceress.

'Very well,' agreed the Wizard. 'Summon them, most noble Glinda.'

18

The Cleverness of Ervic

WE must now return to Ervic the Skeezer, who, when he had set down the copper kettle containing the three fishes at the gate of the lonely cottage, had asked, 'What next?'

The gold fish stuck its head above the water in the kettle and said in its small but distinct voice:

'You are to lift the latch, open the door, and walk boldly into the cottage. Do not be afraid of anything you see, for however you seem to be threatened with dangers, nothing can harm you. The cottage is the home of a powerful Yookoohoo, named Reera the Red, who assumes all sorts of forms, sometimes changing her form several times in a day, according to her fancy. What her real form may be we do not know. This strange creature cannot be bribed with treasure, or coaxed through friendship, or won by pity. She has never assisted anyone, or done wrong to anyone, that we know of. All her wonderful powers are used for her own selfish amusement. She will order you out of the house but you must refuse to go. Remain and watch Reera closely and try to see what she uses to accomplish her transformations. If you can discover the secret whisper it to us and we will then tell you what to do next.'

'That sounds easy,' returned Ervic, who had listened carefully. 'But are you sure she will not hurt me, or try to transform me?'

'She may change your form,' replied the gold fish, 'but do not worry if that happens, for we can break that enchantment easily. You may be sure that nothing will harm you, so you must not be frightened at anything you see or hear.'

Now Ervic was as brave as any ordinary young man, and he knew the fishes who spoke to him were truthful and to be relied upon, nevertheless he experienced a strange sinking of the heart as he picked up the kettle and approached the door of the cottage. His hand trembled as he raised the latch, but he was resolved to obey his instructions. He pushed the door open, took three strides into the middle of the one room the cottage contained, and then stood still and looked around him.

The sights that met his gaze were enough to frighten anyone who had not been properly warned. On the floor just before Ervic lay a great crocodile, its red eyes gleaming wickedly and its wide open mouth displaying rows of sharp teeth. Horned toads hopped about; each of the four upper corners of the room was festooned with a thick cobweb, in the centre of which sat a spider as big round as a washbasin, and armed with pincer-like claws; a red-and-green lizard was stretched at full length on the window-sill and black rats darted in and out of the holes they had gnawed in the floor of the cottage.

But the most startling thing was a huge grey ape which sat upon a bench and knitted. It wore a lace cap, such as old ladies wear, and a little apron of lace, but no other clothing. Its eyes were bright and looked as if coals were burning in them. The ape moved as naturally as an ordinary person might, and on Ervic's entrance stopped knitting and raised its head to look at him.

'Get out!' cried a sharp voice, seeming to come from the ape's mouth.

Ervic saw another bench, empty, just beyond him, so he

stepped over the crocodile, sat down upon the bench and carefully placed the kettle beside him.

'Get out!' again cried the voice.

Ervic shook his head.

'No,' he said, 'I'm going to stay.'

The spiders left their four corners, dropped to the floor and made a rush toward the young Skeezer, circling around his legs with their pincers extended. Ervic paid no attention to them. An enormous black rat ran up Ervic's body, passed around his shoulders and uttered piercing squeals in his ears, but he did not wince. The green-and-red lizard, coming from the window-sill, approached Ervic and began spitting a flaming fluid at him, but Ervic merely stared at the creature and its flame did not touch him.

The crocodile raised its tail and, swinging around, swept Ervic off the bench with a powerful blow. But the Skeezer managed to save the kettle from upsetting and he got up, shook off the horned toads that were crawling over him and resumed his seat on the bench.

All the creatures, after this first attack, remained motionless, as if awaiting orders. The old grey ape knitted on, not looking toward Ervic now, and the young Skeezer stolidly kept his seat. He expected something else to happen, but nothing did. A full hour passed and Ervic was growing nervous.

'What do you want?' the ape asked at last.

'Nothing,' said Ervic.

'You may have that!' retorted the ape, and at this all the strange creatures in the room broke into a chorus of cackling laughter.

Another long wait.

'Do you know who I am?' questioned the ape.

'You must be Reera the Red – the Yookoohoo,' Ervic answered.

'Knowing so much, you must also know that I do not like strangers. Your presence here in my home annoys me. Do you not fear my anger?'

'No,' said the young man.

'Do you intend to obey me, and leave this house?'

'No,' replied Ervic, just as quietly as the Yookoohoo had spoken.

The ape knitted for a long time before resuming the conversation.

'Curiosity,' it said, 'has led to many a man's undoing. I suppose in some way you have learned that I do tricks of magic, and so through curiosity you have come here. You may have been told that I do not injure anyone, so you are bold enough to disobey my commands to go away. You imagine that you may witness some of the rites of witchcraft, and that they may amuse you. Have I spoken truly?'

'Well,' remarked Ervic, who had been pondering on the strange circumstances of his coming here, 'you are right in some ways, but not in others. I am told that you work magic only for your own amusement. That seems to me very selfish. Few people understand magic. I'm told that you are the only real Yookoohoo in all Oz. Why don't you amuse others as well as yourself?'

'What right have you to question my actions?'

'None at all.'

'And you say you are not here to demand any favours of me?'

'For myself I want nothing from you.'

'You are wise in that. I never grant favours.'

'That doesn't worry me,' declared Ervic.

'But you are curious? You hope to witness some of my magic transformations?'

'If you wish to perform any magic, go ahead,' said Ervic. 'It may interest me and it may not. If you'd rather go on with your knitting, it's all the same to me. I am in no hurry at all.'

This may have puzzled Red Reera, but the face beneath the lace cap could show no expression, being covered with hair. Perhaps in all her career the Yookoohoo had never been visited by anyone who, like this young man, asked for nothing, expected nothing, and had no reason for coming except curiosity. This attitude practically disarmed the witch and she began to regard the Skeezer in a more friendly way. She knitted for some time, seemingly in deep thought, and then she arose and walked to a big cupboard that stood against the wall of the room. When the cupboard door was opened Ervic could see a lot of drawers inside, and into one of these drawers – the second from the bottom – Reera thrust a hairy hand.

Until now Ervic could see over the bent form of the ape, but suddenly the form, with its back to him, seemed to straighten up and blot out the cupboard of drawers. The ape had changed to the form of a woman, dressed in the pretty Gillikin costume, and when she turned around he saw that it was a young woman, whose face was quite attractive.

'Do you like me better this way?' Reera inquired with a smile.

'You *look* better,' he said calmly, 'but I'm not sure I *like* you any better.'

She laughed, saying: 'During the heat of the day I like to be an ape, for an ape doesn't wear any clothes to speak of. But if one has gentlemen callers it is proper to dress up.'

Ervic noticed her right hand was closed, as if she held something in it. She shut the cupboard door, bent over the crocodile and in a moment the creature had changed to a red wolf. It was not pretty even now, and the wolf crouched beside its mistress as a dog might have done. Its teeth looked as dangerous as had those of the crocodile.

Next the Yookoohoo went about touching all the lizards and toads, and at her touch they became kittens. The rats she changed into chipmunks. Now the only horrid creatures remaining were the four great spiders, which hid themselves behind their thick webs.

'There!' Reera cried, 'now my cottage presents a more comfortable appearance. I love the toads and lizards and rats, because most people hate them, but I would tire of them if they always remained the same. Sometimes I change their forms a dozen times a day.'

'You are clever,' said Ervic. 'I did not hear you utter any incantations or magic words. All you did was to touch the creatures.'

'Oh, do you think so?' she replied. 'Well, touch them yourself, if you like, and see if you can change their forms.'

'No,' said the Skeezer, 'I don't understand magic and if I did I would not try to imitate your skill. You are a wonderful Yookoohoo, while I am only a common Skeezer.'

This confession seemed to please Reera, who liked to have her witchcraft appreciated.

'Will you go away now?' she asked. 'I prefer to be alone.'

'I prefer to stay here,' said Ervic.

'In another person's home, where you are not wanted?'

'Yes.'

'Is not your curiosity yet satisfied?' demanded Reera, with a smile.

'I don't know. Is there anything else you can do?'

'Many things. But why should I exhibit my powers to a stranger?'

'I can think of no reason at all,' he replied.

She looked at him curiously.

'You want no power for yourself, you say, and you're too

stupid to be able to steal my secrets. This isn't a pretty cottage, while outside are sunshine, broad prairies and beautiful wildflowers. Yet you insist on sitting on that bench and annoying me with your unwelcome presence. What have you in that kettle?'

'Three fishes,' he answered readily.

'Where did you get them?'

'I caught them in the Lake of the Skeezers.'

'What do you intend to do with the fishes?'

'I shall carry them to the home of a friend of mine who has three children. The children will love to have the fishes for pets.'

She came over to the bench and looked into the kettle, where the three fishes were swimming quietly in the water. 'They're pretty,' said Reera. 'Let me transform them into something else.'

'No,' objected the Skeezer.

'I love to transform things; it's so interesting. And I've never transformed any fishes in all my life.'

'Let them alone,' said Ervic.

'What shapes would you prefer them to have? I can make them turtles, or cute little sea-horses; or I could make them piglets, or rabbits, or guinea-pigs; or, if you like I can make chickens of them, or eagles, or bluejays.'

'Let them alone!' repeated Ervic.

'You're not a very pleasant visitor,' laughed Red Reera. 'People accuse *me* of being cross and crabbed and unsociable, and they are quite right. If you had come here pleading and begging for favours, and half afraid of my Yookoohoo magic, I'd have abused you until you ran away; but you're quite different from that. *You're* the unsociable and crabbed and disagreeable one, and so I like you, and bear with your grumpiness. It's time for my midday meal; are you hungry?'

'No,' said Ervic, although he really desired food.

'Well, I am,' Reera declared and clapped her hands together. Instantly a table appeared, spread with linen and bearing dishes of various foods, some smoking hot. There were two plates laid, one at each end of the table, and as soon as Reera seated herself all her creatures gathered around her, as if they were accustomed to be fed when she ate. The wolf squatted at her right hand and the kittens and chipmunks gathered at her left.

'Come, Stranger, sit down and eat,' she called cheerfully, 'and while we're eating let us decide into what forms we shall change your fishes.'

'They're all right as they are,' asserted Ervic, drawing up his bench to the table. 'The fishes are beauties – one gold, one silver and one bronze. Nothing that has life is more lovely than a beautiful fish.'

'What! Am *I* not more lovely?' Reera asked, smiling at his serious face.

'I don't object to you – for a Yookoohoo, you know,' he said, helping himself to the food and eating with good appetite.

'And don't you consider a beautiful girl more lovely than a fish, however pretty the fish may be?'

'Well,' replied Ervic, after a period of thought, 'that might be. If you transformed my three fish into three girls – girls who would be Adepts at Magic, you know they might please me as well as the fish do. You won't do that of course, because you can't, with all your skill. And, should you be able to do so, I fear my troubles would be more than I could bear. They would not consent to be my slaves – especially if they were Adepts at Magic – and so they would command *me* to obey *them*. No, Mistress Reera, let us not transform the fishes at all.'

The Skeezer had put his case with remarkable cleverness. He realized that if he appeared anxious for such a transformation the Yookoohoo would not perform it, yet he had skilfully suggested that they be made Adepts at Magic.

19

Red Reera, the Yookoohoo

AFTER the meal was over and Reera had fed her pets, including the four monster spiders which had come down from their webs to secure their share, she made the table disappear from the floor of the cottage.

'I wish you'd consent to my transforming your fishes,' she said, as she took up her knitting again.

The Skeezer made no reply. He thought it unwise to hurry matters. All during the afternoon they sat silent. Once Reera went to her cupboard and after thrusting her hand into the same drawer as before, touched the wolf and transformed it into a bird with gorgeous coloured feathers. This bird was larger than a parrot and of a somewhat different form, but Ervic had never seen one like it before.

'Sing!' said Reera to the bird, which had perched itself on a big wooden peg – as if it had been in the cottage before and knew just what to do.

And the bird sang jolly, rollicking songs with words to them – just as a person who had been carefully trained might do. The songs were entertaining and Ervic enjoyed listening to them. In an hour or so the bird stopped singing, tucked its head under its wing and went to sleep. Reera continued knitting but seemed thoughtful.

Now Ervic had marked this cupboard drawer well and had concluded that Reera took something from it which enabled her to perform her transformations. He thought that if he managed to remain in the cottage, and Reera fell asleep, he could slyly open the cupboard, take a portion of whatever was in the drawer, and by dropping it into the copper kettle transform the three fishes into their natural shapes. Indeed, he had firmly resolved to carry out this plan when the Yookoohoo put down her knitting and walked toward the door.

'I'm going out for a few minutes,' said she; 'do you wish to go with me, or will you remain here?'

Ervic did not answer but sat quietly on his bench. So Reera went out and closed the cottage door.

As soon as she was gone, Ervic rose and tiptoed to the cupboard.

'Take care! Take care!' cried several voices, coming from the kittens and chipmunks. 'If you touch anything we'll tell the Yookoohoo!'

Ervic hesitated a moment but, remembering that he need not consider Reera's anger if he succeeded in transforming the fishes, he was about to open the cupboard when he was arrested by the voices of the fishes, which stuck their heads above the water in the kettle and called out:

'Come here, Ervic!'

So he went back to the kettle and bent over it.

'Let the cupboard alone,' said the gold fish to him earnestly. 'You could not succeed by getting that magic powder, for only the Yookoohoo knows how to use it. The best way is to allow her to transform us into three girls, for then we will have our natural shapes and be able to perform all the Arts of Magic we have learned and well understand. You are acting wisely and in the most effective manner. We did not know you were so intelligent, or that Reera could be so easily deceived by you. Continue as you have begun and try to persuade her to transform us. But insist that we be given the forms of girls.'

The gold fish ducked its head down just as Reera re-entered the cottage. She saw Eric bent over the kettle, so she came and joined him.

'Can your fishes talk?' she asked.

'Sometimes,' he replied, 'for all fishes in the Land of Oz know how to speak. Just now they were asking me for some bread. They are hungry.'

'Well, they can have some bread,' said Reera. 'But it is nearly supper-time, and if you would allow me to transform your fishes into girls they could join us at the table and have plenty of food much nicer than crumbs. Why not let me transform them?'

'Well,' said Ervic, as if hesitating, 'ask the fishes. If they consent, why – why, then, I'll think it over.'

Reera bent over the kettle and asked:

'Can you hear me, little fishes?'

All three popped their heads above water.

'We can hear you,' said the bronze fish.

'I want to give you other forms, such as rabbits, or turtles or girls, or something; but your master, the surly Skeezer, does not wish me to. However, he has agreed to the plan if you will consent.'

'We'd like to be girls,' said the silver fish.

'No, no!' exclaimed Ervic.

'If you promise to make us three beautiful girls, we will consent,' said the gold fish.

'No, no!' exclaimed Ervic again.

'Also make us Adepts at Magic,' added the bronze fish.

'I don't know exactly what that means,' replied Reera musingly, 'but as no Adept at Magic is as powerful as Yookoohoo, I'll add that to the transformation.'

'We won't try to harm you, or to interfere with your magic in any way,' promised the gold fish. 'On the contrary, we will be your friends.'

'Will you agree to go away and leave me alone in my

cottage, whenever I command you to do so?' asked Reera.

'We promise that,' cried the three fishes.

'Don't do it! Don't consent to the transformation,' urged Ervic.

'They have already consented,' said the Yookoohoo, laughing in his face, 'and you have promised me to abide by their decision. So, friend Skeezer, I shall perform the transformation whether you like it or not.'

Ervic seated himself on the bench again, a deep scowl on his face but joy in his heart. Reera moved over to the cupboard, took something from the drawer and returned to the copper kettle. She was clutching something tightly in her right hand, but with her left she reached within the kettle, took out the three fishes and laid them carefully on the floor, where they gasped in distress at being out of water.

Reera did not keep them in misery more than a few seconds, for she touched each one with her right hand and instantly the fishes were transformed into three tall and slender young women, with fine, intelligent faces and clothed in handsome, clinging gowns. The one who had been a gold fish had beautiful golden hair and blue eyes and was exceedingly fair of skin; the one who had been a bronze fish had dark brown hair and clear grey eyes and her complexion matched these lovely features. The one who had been a silver fish had snow-white hair of the finest texture and deep brown eyes. The hair contrasted exquisitely with her pink cheeks and ruby-red lips, nor did it make her look a day older than her two companions.

As soon as they secured these girlish shapes, all three bowed low to the Yookoohoo and said:

'We thank you, Reera.'

Then they bowed to the Skeezer and said:

'We thank you, Ervic.'

'Very good!' cried the Yookoohoo, examining her work

with critical approval. 'You are much better and more interesting than fishes, and this ungracious Skeezer would scarcely allow me to do the transformations. You surely have nothing to thank *him* for. But now let us dine in honour of the occasion.'

She clapped her hands together and again a table loaded with food appeared in the cottage. It was a longer table, this time, and places were set for the three Adepts as well as for Reera and Ervic.

'Sit down, friends, and eat your fill,' said the Yookoohoo, but instead of seating herself at the head of the table she went to the cupboard, saying to the Adepts: 'Your beauty and grace, my fair friends, quite outshine my own. So that I may appear properly at the banquet table I intend, in honour of this occasion, to take upon myself my natural shape.'

Scarcely had she finished this speech when Reera transformed herself into a young woman fully as lovely as the three Adepts. She was not quite so tall as they, but her form was more rounded and more handsomely clothed, with a wonderful jewelled girdle and a necklace of shining pearls. Her hair was a bright auburn red, and her eyes large and dark.

'Do you claim this is your natural form?' asked Ervic of the Yookoohoo.

'Yes,' she replied. 'This is the only form I am really entitled to wear. But I seldom assume it because there is no one here to admire or appreciate it and I get tired admiring it myself.'

'I see now why you are named Reera the Red,' remarked Ervic.

'It is on account of my red hair,' she explained smiling. 'I do not care for red hair myself, which is one reason I usually wear other forms.'

'It is beautiful,' asserted the young man; and then remembering the other women present he added: 'But of course, all women should not have red hair, because that would make it too common. Gold and silver and brown hair are equally handsome.'

The smiles that he saw interchanged between the four filled the poor Skeezer with embarrassment, so he fell silent and attended to eating his supper, leaving the others to do the talking. The three Adepts frankly told Reera who they were, how they became fishes and how they had planned secretly to induce the Yookoohoo to transform them. They admitted that they had feared, had they asked her to help, that she would have refused them.

'You were quite right,' returned the Yookoohoo. 'I make it my rule never to perform magic to assist others, for if I did there would always be crowds at my cottage demanding help and I hate crowds and want to be left alone.

'However, now that you are restored to your proper shapes, I do not regret my action and I hope you will be of use in saving the Skeezer people by raising their island to the surface of the lake, where it really belongs. But you must promise me that after you go away you will never come here again, nor tell anyone what I have done for you.'

The three Adepts and Ervic thanked the Yookoohoo warmly. They promised to remember her wish that they should not come to her cottage again and so, with a good-bye, took their departure.

20

A Puzzling Problem

GLINDA THE GOOD, having decided to try her sorcery upon
the abandoned submarine, so that it would obey her commands, asked all of her party, including the Skeezers, to
withdraw from the shore of the lake to the line of palm trees.
She kept with her only the little Wizard of Oz, who was her
pupil and knew how to assist her in her magic rites. When
they two were alone beside the stranded boat, Glinda said
to the Wizard:

'I shall first try my magic recipe No. 1163, which is
intended to make inanimate objects move at my command.
Have you a skeropythrope with you?'

'Yes, I always carry one in my bag,' replied the Wizard.
He opened his black bag of magic tools and took out a
brightly polished skeropythrope, which he handed to the
Sorceress. Glinda had also brought a small wicker bag,
containing various requirements of sorcery, and from this
she took a parcel of powder and a vial of liquid. She poured
the liquid into the skeropythrope and added the powder. At
once the skeropythrope began to sputter and emit sparks of a
violet colour, which spread in all directions. The Sorceress
instantly stepped into the middle of the boat and held the
instrument so that the sparks fell all around her and covered
every bit of the blackened steel boat. At the same time Glinda
crooned a weird incantation in the language of sorcery,
her voice sounding low and musical.

After a little the violet sparks ceased, and those that had
fallen upon the boat had disappeared and left no mark upon
its surface. The ceremony was ended and Glinda returned

the skeropythrope to the Wizard, who put it away in his black bag.

'That ought to do the business all right,' he said confidently.

'Let us make a trial and see,' she replied.

So they both entered the boat and seated themselves.

Speaking in a tone of command the Sorceress said to the boat: 'Carry us across the lake, to the farther shore.'

At once the boat backed off the sandy beach, turned its prow and moved swiftly over the water.

'Very good – very good indeed!' cried the Wizard, when the boat slowed up at the shore opposite from that whence they had departed. 'Even Coo-ee-oh, with all her witchcraft, could do no better.'

The Sorceress now said to the boat:

'Close up, submerge and carry us to the basement door of the sunken island – the door from which you emerged at the command of Queen Coo-ee-oh.'

The boat obeyed. As it sank into the water the top sections rose from the sides and joined together over the heads of Glinda and the Wizard, who were thus enclosed in a waterproof chamber. There were four glass windows in this covering, one on each side and one on either end, so that the passengers could see exactly where they were going. Moving under water more slowly than on the surface, the submarine gradually approached the island and halted with its bow pressed against the huge marble door in the basement under the Dome. This door was tightly closed and it was evident to both Glinda and the Wizard that it would not open to admit the underwater boat unless a magic word was spoken by them or someone from within the basement of the island. But what was this magic word? Neither of them knew.

'I'm afraid,' said the Wizard regretfully, 'that we can't get in, after all. Unless your sorcery can discover the word to open the marble door.'

'That is probably some word only known to Coo-ee-oh,' replied the Sorceress. 'I may be able to discover what it is, but that will require time. Let us go back again to our companions.'

'It seems a shame, after we have made the boat obey us, to be balked by just a marble door,' grumbled the Wizard.

At Glinda's command the boat rose until it was on a level with the glass dome that covered the Skeezer village, when the Sorceress made it slowly circle all around the Great Dome.

Many faces were pressed against the glass from the inside, eagerly watching the submarine, and in one place were Dorothy and Ozma, who quickly recognized Glinda and the Wizard through the glass windows of the boat. Glinda saw them, too, and held the boat close to the Dome while the friends exchanged greetings in pantomime. Their voices, unfortunately, could not be heard through the Dome and the water and the side of the boat. The Wizard tried to make the girls understand, through signs, that he and Glinda had come to their rescue, and Ozma and Dorothy understood this from the very fact that the Sorceress and the Wizard had appeared. The two girl prisoners were smiling and in safety, and knowing this Glinda felt she could take all the time necessary in order to effect their final rescue.

As nothing more could be done just then, Glinda ordered the boat to return to shore, and it obeyed readily. First it ascended to the surface of the water, then the roof parted and fell into the slots at the side of the boat, and then the magic craft quickly made the shore and beached itself on the sands at the very spot from which it had departed at Glinda's command.

All the Oz people and the Skeezers at once ran to the boat to ask if they had reached the island, and whether they had seen Ozma and Dorothy. The Wizard told them of the obstacle they had met in the way of a marble door, and how Glinda would now undertake to find a magic way to conquer the door.

Realizing that it would require several days to succeed in reaching the island, raising it and liberating their friends and the Skeezer people, Glinda now prepared a camp half-way between the lake shore and the palm trees.

The Wizard's wizardry made a number of tents appear and the sorcery of the Sorceress furnished these tents all complete, with beds, chairs, tables, rugs, lamps and even books with which to pass idle hours. All the tents had the Royal Banner of Oz flying from the centrepoles and one big tent, not now occupied, had Ozma's own banner moving in the breeze.

Betsy and Trot had a tent to themselves, and Button Bright and Ojo had another. The Scarecrow and the Tin Woodman paired together in one tent and so did Jack Pumpkinhead and the Shaggy Man, Cap'n Bill and Uncle Henry, Tik-Tok and Professor Wogglebug. Glinda had the most splendid tent of all, except that reserved for Ozma, while the Wizard had a little one of his own. Whenever it was meal time, tables loaded with food magically appeared in the tents of those who were in the habit of eating, and these complete arrangements made the rescue party just as comfortable as they would have been in their own homes.

Far into the night Glinda sat in her tent studying a roll of mystic scrolls in search of a word that would open the basement door of the island and admit her to the Great Dome. She also made many magical experiments, hoping to discover something that would aid her. Yet the morning found the powerful Sorceress still unsuccessful.

Glinda's art could have opened any ordinary door, you may be sure, but you must realize that this marble door of the island had been commanded not to open save in obedi-

ence to one magic word, and therefore all other magic
words could have no effect upon it. The magic word that
guarded the door had probably been invented by Coo-ee-oh,
who had now forgotten it. The only way, then, to gain
entrance to the sunken island was to break the charm that
held the door fast shut. If this could be done no magic would
be required to open it.

The next day the Sorceress and the Wizard again entered
the boat and made it submerge and go to the marble door,
which they tried in various ways to open, but without
success.

'We shall have to abandon this attempt, I think,' said
Glinda. 'The easiest way to raise the island would be for us
to gain admittance to the Dome and then descend to the
basement and see in what manner Coo-ee-oh made the
entire island sink or rise at her command. It naturally
occurred to me that the easiest way to gain admittance
would be by having the boat take us into the basement
through the marble door from which Coo-ee-oh launched it.
But there must be other ways to get inside the Dome and
join Ozma and Dorothy, and such ways we must find by
study and the proper use of our powers of magic.'

'It won't be easy,' declared the Wizard, 'for we must not
forget that Ozma herself understands considerable magic,
and has doubtless tried to raise the island or find other means
of escape from it and failed.'

'That is true,' returned Glinda, 'but Ozma's magic is
fairy magic, while you are a Wizard and I am a Sorceress.
In this way the three of us have a great variety of magic to
work with, and if we should all fail it will be because the
island is raised and lowered by a magic power none of us is
acquainted with. My idea therefore is to seek – by such
magic as we possess – to accomplish our object in another
way.'

They made the circle of the Dome again in their boat, and once more saw Ozma and Dorothy through their windows and exchanged signals with the two imprisoned girls.

Ozma realized that her friends were doing all in their power to rescue her and smiled an encouragement to their efforts. Dorothy seemed a little anxious but was trying to be as brave as her companion.

After the boat had returned to the camp and Glinda was seated in her tent, working out various ways by which Ozma and Dorothy could be rescued, the Wizard stood on the shore dreamily eyeing the outlines of the Great Dome which showed beneath the clear water, when he raised his eyes and saw a group of strange people approaching from around the lake. Three were young women of stately presence, very beautifully dressed, who moved with remarkable grace. They were followed at a little distance by a good-looking young Skeezer.

The Wizard saw at a glance that these people might be very important, so he advanced to meet them. The three maidens received him graciously and the one with the golden hair said:

'I believe you are the famous Wizard of Oz, of whom I have often heard. We are seeking Glinda, the Sorceress, and perhaps you can lead us to her.'

'I can, and will, right gladly,' answered the Wizard. 'Follow me, please.'

The little Wizard was puzzled as to the identity of the three lovely visitors but he gave no sign that might embarrass them.

He understood they did not wish to be questioned, and so he made no remarks as he led the way to Glinda's tent.

With a courtly bow the Wizard ushered the three visitors into the gracious presence of Glinda, the Good.

21

The Three Adepts

THE Sorceress looked up from her work as the three maidens entered, and something in their appearance and manner led her to rise and bow to them in her most dignified manner. The three knelt an instant before the great Sorceress and then stood upright and waited for her to speak.

'Whoever you may be,' said Glinda, 'I bid you welcome.'

'My name is Audah,' said one.

'My name is Aurah,' said another.

'My name is Aujah,' said the third.

Glinda had never heard these names before, but looking closely at the three she asked:

'Are you witches or workers in magic?'

'Some of the secret arts we have gleaned from Nature,' replied the brown-haired maiden modestly, 'but we do not place our skill beside that of the great Sorceress, Glinda the Good.'

'I suppose you are aware it is unlawful to practise magic in the Land of Oz, without the permission of our Ruler, Princess Ozma?'

'No, we were not aware of that,' was the reply. 'We have heard of Ozma, who is the appointed Ruler of all this great fairyland, but her laws have not reached us as yet.'

Glinda studied the strange maidens thoughtfully; then she said to them:

'Princess Ozma is even now imprisoned in the Skeezer village, for the whole island with its Great Dome, was sunk to the bottom of the lake by the witchcraft of Coo-ee-oh, whom the Flathead Su-dic transformed into a silly swan. I am seeking some way to overcome Coo-ee-oh's magic and raise the isle to the surface again. Can you help me do this?'

The maidens exchanged glances, and the white-haired one replied:

'We do not know; but we will try to assist you.'

'It seems,' continued Glinda musingly, 'that Coo-ee-oh derived most of her witchcraft from three Adepts at Magic, who at one time ruled the Flatheads. While the Adepts were being entertained by Coo-ee-oh at a banquet in her palace, she cruelly betrayed them and after transforming them into fishes cast them into the lake.

'If I could find these three fishes and return them to their natural shapes – they might know what magic Coo-ee-oh used to sink the island. I was about to go to the shore and call these fishes to me when you arrived. So, if you will join me, we will try to find them.'

The maidens exchanged smiles now, and the golden-haired one, Audah, said to Glinda:

'It will not be necessary to go to the lake. We are the three fishes.'

'Indeed!' cried Glinda. 'Then you are the three Adepts at Magic, restored to your proper forms?'

'We are the three Adepts,' admitted Aujah.

'Then,' said Glinda, 'my task is half accomplished. But who destroyed the transformation that made you fishes?'

'We have promised not to tell,' answered Aurah; 'but this young Skeezer was largely responsible for our release; he is brave and clever, and we owe him our gratitude.'

Glinda looked at Ervic, who stood modestly behind the Adepts, hat in hand. 'He shall be properly rewarded,' she declared, 'for in helping you he has helped us all, and perhaps saved his people from being imprisoned for ever in the sunken isle.'

The Sorceress now asked her guests to seat themselves and a long talk followed, in which the Wizard of Oz shared.

'We are quite certain,' said Aurah, 'that if we could get inside the Dome we could discover Coo-ee-oh's secrets, for in all her work, after we became fishes, she used the formulas and incantations and arts that she stole from us. She may have added to these things, but they were the foundation of all her work.'

'What means do you suggest for our getting into the Dome?' inquired Glinda.

The three Adepts hesitated to reply, for they had not yet considered what could be done to reach the inside of the Great Dome. While they were in deep thought, and Glinda and the Wizard were quietly awaiting their suggestions, into the tent rushed Trot and Betsy, dragging between them the Patchwork Girl.

'Oh, Glinda,' cried Trot, 'Scraps has thought of a way to rescue Ozma and Dorothy and all of the Skeezers.'

The three Adepts could not avoid laughing merrily, for not only were they amused by the queer form of the Patchwork Girl, but Trot's enthusiastic speech struck them as really funny. If the Great Sorceress and the famous Wizard and the three talented Adepts at Magic were unable as yet to solve the important problem of the sunken isle, there was little chance for a patched girl stuffed with cotton to succeed.

But Glinda, smiling indulgently at the earnest faces turned toward her, patted the children's heads and said:

'Scraps is very clever. Tell us what she has thought of, my dear.'

'Well,' said Trot, 'Scraps says that if you could dry up all the water in the lake the island would be on dry land, an' everyone could come and go whenever they liked.'

Glinda smiled again, but the Wizard said to the girls:

'If we should dry up the lake, what would become of all the beautiful fishes that now live in the water?'

'Dear me! That's so,' admitted Betsy, crestfallen; 'we never thought of that, did we Trot?'

'Couldn't you transform 'em into polliwogs?' asked Scraps, turning a somersault and then standing on one leg.

'You could give them a little, teeny pond to swim in, and they'd be just as happy as they are as fishes.'

'No indeed!' replied the Wizard, severely. 'It is wicked to transform any living creatures without their consent, and the lake is the home of the fishes and belongs to them.'

'All right,' said Scraps, making a face at him; 'I don't care.'

'It's too bad,' sighed Trot, 'for I thought we'd struck a splendid idea.'

'So you did,' declared Glinda, her face now grave and thoughtful. 'There is something in the Patchwork Girl's idea that may be of real value to us.'

'I think so, too,' agreed the golden-haired Adept. 'The top of the Great Dome is only a few feet below the surface of the water. If we could reduce the level of the lake until the Dome sticks a little above the water, we could remove some of the glass and let ourselves down into the village by means of ropes.'

'And there would be plenty of water left for the fishes to swim in,' added the white-haired maiden.

'If we succeed in raising the island we could fill up the lake again,' suggested the brown-haired Adept.

'I believe,' said the Wizard, rubbing his hands together in delight, 'that the Patchwork Girl has shown us the way to success.'

The girls were looking curiously at the three beautiful Adepts, wondering who they were, so Glinda introduced them to Trot and Betsy and Scraps, and then sent the children away while she considered how to carry the new idea into effect.

Not much could be done that night, so the Wizard prepared another tent for the Adepts, and in the evening Glinda held a reception and invited all her followers to meet the new arrivals. The Adepts were greatly astonished at the extraordinary personages presented to them, and marvelled that Jack Pumpkinhead and the Scarecrow and the Tin Woodman and Tik-Tok could really live and think and talk just like other people. They were especially pleased with the lively Patchwork Girl and loved to watch her antics.

It was quite a pleasant party, for Glinda served some dainty refreshments to those who could eat, and the Scarecrow recited some poems, and the Cowardly Lion sang a song in his deep bass voice. The only thing that marred their joy was the thought that their beloved Ozma and dear little Dorothy were yet confined in the Great Dome of the Sunken Island.

22

The Sunken Island

As soon as they had breakfasted the next morning, Glinda and the Wizard and the three Adepts went down to the shore of the lake and formed a line with their faces toward the submerged island. All the others came to watch them, but stood at a respectful distance in the background.

At the right of the Sorceress stood Audah and Aurah, while at the left stood the Wizard and Aujah. Together they stretched their arms over the water's edge and in unison the five chanted a rhythmic incantation.

This chant they repeated again and again, swaying their arms gently from side to side, and in a few minutes the watchers behind them noticed that the lake had begun to recede from the shore. Before long the highest point of the dome appeared above the water. Gradually the water fell, making the dome appear to rise. When it was three or four feet above the surface Glinda gave the signal to stop, for their work had been accomplished.

The blackened submarine was now entirely out of water, but Uncle Henry and Cap'n Bill managed to push it into the lake. Glinda, the Wizard, Ervic and the Adepts got into the boat, taking with them a coil of strong rope, and at the command of the Sorceress the craft cleaved its way through the water towards the part of the Dome which was now visible.

'There's still plenty of water for the fish to swim in,' observed the Wizard as they rode along. 'They might like more but I'm sure they can get along until we have raised the island and can fill up the lake again.'

The boat touched gently on the sloping glass of the Dome, and the Wizard took some tools from his black bag and quickly removed one large pane of glass, thus making a hole large enough for their bodies to pass through. Stout frames of steel supported the glass of the Dome, and around one of these frames the Wizard tied the end of a rope.

'I'll go down first,' said he, 'for while I'm not as spry as Cap'n Bill I'm sure I can manage it easily. Are you sure the rope is long enough to reach the bottom?'

'Quite sure,' replied the Sorceress.

So the Wizard let down the rope and climbing through the opening lowered himself down, hand over hand, clinging to the rope with his legs and feet. Below in the streets of the village were gathered all the Skeezers, men, women and children, and you may be sure that Ozma and Dorothy, with Lady Aurex, were filled with joy that their friends were at last coming to their rescue.

The Queen's palace, now occupied by Ozma, was directly in the centre of the Dome, so that when the rope was let down the end of it came just in front of the palace entrance. Several Skeezers held fast to the rope's end to steady it and the Wizard reached the ground in safety. He hugged first Ozma and then Dorothy, while all the Skeezers cheered as loud as they could.

The Wizard now discovered that the rope was long enough to reach from the top of the Dome to the ground when doubled, so he tied a chair to one end of the rope and called to Glinda to sit in the chair while he and some of the Skeezers lowered her to the pavement. In this way the Sorceress reached the ground quite comfortably and the three Adepts and Ervic soon followed her.

The Skeezers quickly recognized the three Adepts at Magic, whom they had learned to respect before their wicked Queen betrayed them, and welcomed them as friends. All the inhabitants of the village had been greatly frightened by their imprisonment under water, but now realized that an attempt was to be made to rescue them.

Glinda, the Wizard and the Adepts followed Ozma and Dorothy into the palace, and they asked Lady Aurex and Ervic to join them. After Ozma had told of her adventures in trying to prevent war between the Flatheads and the Skeezers, and Glinda had told all about the Rescue Expedition and the restoration of the three Adepts by the help of Ervic, a serious consultation was held as to how the island could be made to rise.

'I've tried every way in my power,' said Ozma, 'but Coo-ee-oh used a very unusual sort of magic which I do not understand. She seems to have prepared her witchcraft in such a way that a spoken word is necessary to accomplish her designs, and these spoken words are known only to herself.'

'That is a method we taught her,' declared Aurah the Adept.

'I can do no more, Glinda,' continued Ozma, 'so I wish you would try what your sorcery can accomplish.'

'First, then,' said Glinda, 'let us visit the basement of the island, which I am told is underneath the village.'

A flight of marble stairs led from one of Coo-ee-oh's private rooms down to the basement, but when the party arrived all were puzzled by what they saw. In the centre of a broad, low room, stood a mass of great cog-wheels, chains and pulleys, all interlocked and seeming to form a huge machine; but there was no engine or other motive power to make the wheels turn.

'This, I suppose, is the means by which the island is lowered or raised,' said Ozma, 'but the magic word which is needed to move the machinery is unknown to us.'

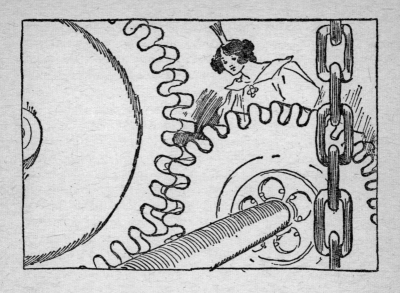

The three Adepts were carefully examining the mass of wheels, and soon the golden-haired one said:

'These wheels do not control the island at all. On the contrary, one set of them is used to open the doors of the little rooms where the submarines are kept, as may be seen from the chains and pulleys used. Each boat is kept in a little room with two doors, one to the basement room where we are now and the other letting into the lake.

'When Coo-ee-oh used the boat in which she attacked the Flatheads, she first commanded the basement door to open and with her followers she got into the boat and made the top close over them. Then the basement door being closed, the outer door was slowly opened, letting the water fill the room to float the boat, which then left the island, keeping under water.'

'But how could she expect to get back again?' asked the Wizard.

'Why the boat would enter the room filled with water and after the outer door was closed a word of command started a pump which pumped all the water from the room. Then the boat would open and Coo-ee-oh could enter the basement.'

'I see,' said the Wizard. 'It is a clever contrivance, but won't work unless one knows the magic words.'

'Another part of this machinery,' explained the white-haired Adept, 'is used to extend the bridge from the island to the mainland. The steel bridge is in a room much like that in which the boats are kept, and at Coo-ee-oh's command it would reach out, joint by joint, until its far end touched the shore of the lake. The same magic command would make the bridge return to its former position. Of course the bridge could not be used unless the island was on the surface of the water.'

'But how do you suppose Coo-ee-oh managed to sink the island, and make it rise again?' inquired Glinda.

This the Adepts could not yet explain. As nothing more could be learned from the basement they mounted the steps to the Queen's private suite again, and Ozma showed them to a special room where Coo-ee-oh kept her magical instruments and performed all her arts of witchcraft.

23

The Magic Words

MANY interesting things were to be seen in the Room of Magic, including much that had been stolen from the Adepts when they were transformed to fishes, but they had to admit that Coo-ee-oh had a rare genius for mechanics, and had used her knowledge in inventing a lot of mechanical apparatus that ordinary witches, wizards and sorcerers could not understand.

They all carefully inspected this room, taking care to examine every article they came across.

'The island,' said Glinda thoughtfully, 'rests on a base of solid marble. When it is submerged, as it is now, the base of the island is upon the bottom of the lake. What puzzles me is how such a great weight can be lifted and suspended in the water, even by magic.'

'I now remember,' returned Aujah, 'that one of the arts we taught Coo-ee-oh was the way to expand steel, and I think that explains how the island is raised and lowered. I noticed in the basement a big steel pillar that passed through the floor and extended upward to this place. Perhaps the end of it is concealed in this very room. If the lower end of the steel pillar is firmly embedded in the bottom of the lake, Coo-ee-oh could utter a magic word that would make the pillar expand, and so lift the entire island to the level of the water.'

'I've found the end of the steel pillar. It's just here,' announced the Wizard, pointing to one side of the room where a great basin of polished steel seemed to have been set upon the floor.

They all gathered around, and Ozma said:

'Yes, I am quite sure that is the upper end of the pillar that supports the island. I noticed it when I first came here. It has been hollowed out, you see, and something has been burned in the basin, for the fire has left its marks. I wondered what was under the great basin and got several of the Skeezers to come up here and try to lift it for me. They were strong men, but could not move it at all.'

'It seems to me,' said Audah the Adept, 'that we have discovered the manner in which Coo-ee-oh raised the island. She would burn some sort of magic powder in the basin, utter the magic word, and the pillar would lengthen out and lift the island with it.'

'What's this?' asked Dorothy, who had been searching around with the others, and now noticed a slight hollow in the wall, near to where the steel basin stood. As she spoke Dorothy pushed her thumb into the hollow and instantly a small drawer popped out from the wall.

The three Adepts, Glinda and the Wizard sprang forward and peered into the drawer. It was half filled with a greyish powder, the tiny grains of which constantly moved as if impelled by some living force.

'It may be some kind of radium,' said the Wizard.

'No,' replied Glinda, 'it is more wonderful than even radium, for I recognize it as a rare mineral powder called Gaulau by the sorcerers. I wonder how Coo-ee-oh discovered it and where she obtained it.'

'There is no doubt,' said Aujah the Adept, 'that this is the magic powder Coo-ee-oh burned in the basin. If only we knew the magic word, I am quite sure we could raise the island.'

'How can we discover the magic word?' asked Ozma, turning to Glinda as she spoke.

'That we must now seriously consider,' answered the Sorceress.

So all of them sat down in the Room of Magic and began to think. It was so still that after a while Dorothy grew nervous. The little girl never could keep silent for long, and at the risk of displeasing her magic-working friends she suddenly said:

'Well, Coo-ee-oh used just three magic words, one to make the bridge work, and one to make the submarines go out of their holes, and one to raise and lower the island. Three words. And Coo-ee-oh's name is made up of just three words. One is "Coo", and one is "ee", and one is "oh".'

The Wizard frowned but Glinda looked wonderingly at the young girl and Ozma cried out:

'A good thought, Dorothy dear! You may have solved our problem.'

'I believe it is worth a trial,' agreed Glinda. 'It would be quite natural for Coo-ee-oh to divide her name into three magic syllables, and Dorothy's suggestion seems like an inspiration.'

The three Adepts also approved the trial but the brown-haired one said:

'We must be careful not to use the wrong word, and send the bridge out under water. The main thing, if Dorothy's idea is correct, is to hit upon the one word that moves the island.'

'Let us experiment,' suggested the Wizard.

In the drawer with the moving grey powder was a tiny golden cup, which they thought was used for measuring. Glinda filled this cup with the powder and carefully poured it into the shallow basin, which was the top of the great steel pillar supporting the island. Then Aurah the Adept lighted a taper and touched it to the powder, which instantly glowed fiery red and tumbled about the basin with astonishing energy. While the grains of powder still glowed red the Sorceress bent over it and said in a voice of command: 'Coo!'

They waited motionless to see what would happen. There was a grating noise and a whirl of machinery, but the island did not move a particle.

Dorothy rushed to the window, which overlooked the glass side of the dome.

'The boats!' she exclaimed. 'The boats are all loose an' sailing under water.'

'We've made a mistake,' said the Wizard gloomily.

'But it's one which shows we are on the right track,' declared Aujah the Adept. 'We know now that Coo-ee-oh used the syllables of her name for the magic words.'

'If "Coo" sends out the boats, it is probable that "ee" works the bridge,' suggested Ozma. 'So the last part of the name may raise the island.'

'Let us try that next then,' proposed the Wizard.

He scraped the embers of the burned powder out of the basin and Glinda again filled the golden cup from the drawer and placed it on top of the steel pillar. Aurah lighted it with her taper and Ozma bent over the basin and murmured the long drawn syllable: 'Oh-h-h!'

Instantly the island trembled and with a weird groaning noise it moved upward – slowly, very slowly, but with a steady motion, while all the company stood by in awed silence. It was a wonderful thing, even to those skilled in the arts of magic, wizardry and sorcery, to realize that a single word could raise that great, heavy island, with its immense glass Dome.

'Why, we're way *above* the lake now!' exclaimed Dorothy from the window, when at last the island ceased to move.

'That is because we lowered the level of the water,' explained Glinda.

They could hear the Skeezers cheering lustily in the streets of the village as they realized that they were saved.

'Come,' said Ozma eagerly, 'let us go down and join the people.'

'Not just yet,' returned Glinda, a happy smile upon her lovely face, for she was overjoyed at their success. 'First let us extend the bridge to the mainland, where our friends from the Emerald City are waiting.'

It didn't take long to put more powder in the basin, light it and utter the syllable 'EE!' The result was that a door in the basement opened and the steel bridge moved out, extended itself joint by joint, and finally rested its far end on the shore of the lake just in front of the encampment.

'Now,' said Glinda, 'we can go up and receive the congratulations of the Skeezers and of our friends of the Rescue Expedition.'

Across the water, on the shore of the lake, the Patchwork Girl was waving them a welcome.

24

Glinda's Triumph

OF course all those who had joined Glinda's expedition at once crossed the bridge to the island, where they were warmly welcomed by the Skeezers. Before all the concourse of people Princess Ozma made a speech from a porch of the palace and demanded that they recognize her as their lawful Ruler and promise to obey the laws of the Land of Oz. In return she agreed to protect them from all future harm and declared they would no longer be subjected to cruelty and abuse.

This pleased the Skeezers greatly, and when Ozma told them they might elect a Queen to rule over them, who in turn would be subject to Ozma of Oz, they voted for Lady Aurex, and that same day the ceremony of crowning the new Queen was held and Aurex was installed as mistress of the palace.

For her Prime Minister the Queen selected Ervic, for the three Adepts had told of his good judgment, faithfulness and cleverness, and all the Skeezers approved the appointment.

Glinda, the Wizard and the Adepts stood on the bridge and recited an incantation that quite filled the lake with water again, and the Scarecrow and the Patchwork Girl climbed to the top of the Great Dome and replaced the pane of glass that had been removed to allow Glinda and her followers to enter.

When evening came Ozma ordered a great feast prepared, to which every Skeezer was invited. The village was beautifully decorated and brilliantly lighted and there was music and dancing until a late hour to celebrate the liberation of the people. For the Skeezers had been freed, not only from the water of the lake but from the cruelty of their former Queen.

As the people from the Emerald City prepared the next morning to depart Queen Aurex said to Ozma:

'There is only one thing I now fear for my people, and that is the enmity of the terrible Su-dic of the Flatheads. He is liable to come here at any time and try to annoy us, and my Skeezers are peaceful folks and unable to fight the wild and wilful Flatheads.'

'Do not worry,' returned Ozma, reassuringly. 'We intend to stop on our way at the Flatheads' Enchanted Mountain and punish the Su-dic for his misdeeds.'

That satisfied Aurex and when Ozma and her followers trooped over the bridge to the shore, having taken leave of their friends, all the Skeezers cheered them and waved their hats and handkerchiefs, and the band played and the departure was indeed a ceremony long to be remembered.

The three Adepts at Magic, who had formerly ruled the Flatheads wisely and considerately, went with Princess Ozma and her people, for they had promised Ozma to stay on the mountain and again see that the laws were enforced.

Glinda had been told all about the curious Flatheads and she had consulted with the Wizard and formed a plan to render them more intelligent and agreeable.

When the party reached the mountain Ozma and Dorothy showed them how to pass around the invisible wall – which had been built by the Flatheads after the Adepts were transformed – and how to gain the up-and-down stairway that led to the mountain top.

The Su-dic had watched the approach of the party from

the edge of the mountain and was frightened when he saw
that the three Adepts had recovered their natural forms and
were coming back to their former home. He realized that
his power would soon be gone and yet he determined to
fight to the last. He called all the Flatheads together and
armed them, and told them to arrest all who came up the
stairway and hurl them over the edge of the mountain to the
plain below. But although they feared the Supreme Dictator,
who had threatened to punish them if they did not obey his
commands, as soon as they saw the three Adepts they threw
down their arms and begged their former rulers to protect
them.

The three Adepts assured the excited Flatheads that they
had nothing to fear.

Seeing that his people had rebelled the Su-dic ran away
and tried to hide, but the Adepts found him and had him
cast into a prison, all his cans of brains being taken away
from him.

After this easy conquest of the Su-dic, Glinda told the
Adepts of her plan, which had already been approved by
Ozma of Oz, and they joyfully agreed to it. So, during the
next few days, the great Sorceress transformed, in a way,
every Flathead on the mountain.

Taking them one at a time, she had the can of brains that
belonged to each one opened and the contents spread on the
flat head, after which, by means of her arts of sorcery, she
caused the head to grow over the brains – in the manner
most people wear them – and they were thus rendered as
intelligent and good looking as any of the other inhabitants
of the Land of Oz.

When all had been treated in this manner there were no
more Flatheads at all, and the Adepts decided to name their
people Mountaineers. One good result of Glinda's sorcery
was that no one could now be deprived of the brains that

belonged to him and each person had exactly the share he was entitled to.

Even the Su-dic was given his portion of brains and his flat head made round, like the others, but he was deprived of all power to work further mischief, and with the Adepts constantly watching him he would be forced to become obedient and humble.

The Golden Pig, which ran grunting about the streets, with no brains at all, was disenchanted by Glinda, and in her woman's form was given brains and a round head. This wife of the Su-dic had once been even more wicked than her evil husband, but she had now forgotten all her wickedness and was likely to be a good woman thereafter.

These things being accomplished in a satisfactory manner, Princess Ozma and her people bade farewell to the three Adepts and departed for the Emerald City, well pleased with their interesting adventures.

They returned by the road over which Ozma and Dorothy had come, stopping to get the Sawhorse and the Red Wagon where they had left them.

'I'm very glad I went to see these peoples,' said Princess Ozma, 'for I not only prevented any further warfare between them, but they have been freed from the rule of the Su-dic and Coo-ee-oh and are now happy and loyal subjects of the Land of Oz. Which proves that it is always wise to do one's duty, however unpleasant that duty may seem to be.'

Armada

This is a special Larger Size Armada Book for Younger Children. Have you read the others in the series? They're all full of exciting stories and fun, with lovely colourful jackets. Start your collection now!

The Wizard of Oz · The Marvellous Land of Oz
Glinda of Oz

by L. Frank Baum

The strange and wonderful adventures of Dorothy from Kansas in the magic land of Oz

The Shoeshop Bears · Hannibal and the Bears

by Margaret J. Baker

The first two stories in a series about three very exceptional teddybears will delight imaginative children everywhere

Mermaids and Sea Monsters · Witches · Animal Ghosts

by Carolyn Lloyd

Three collections of all sorts of fascinating stories, poems, legends and pictures. Some wierd and mysterious, some funny, some frightening – there are lots of surprises when you turn the pages!

Holiday House · Picnic Party
Storytime Book · Happy Days Stories
Rainy Day Stories

by Enid Blyton

Five books jam-packed with stories from a much-loved author. Hundreds of splendid characters and tales for many happy reading hours

MARVEL

GUARDIANS OF THE GALAXY

MAD LIBS®

by Paula K. Manzanero

Mad Libs
An Imprint of Penguin Random House

MAD LIBS®

INSTRUCTIONS

MAD LIBS® is a game for people who don't like games!
It can be played by one, two, three, four, or forty.

● RIDICULOUSLY SIMPLE DIRECTIONS

In this tablet you will find stories containing blank spaces where words
are left out. One player, the READER, selects one of these stories. The
READER does not tell anyone what the story is about. Instead, he/she asks
the other players, the WRITERS, to give him/her words. These words are
used to fill in the blank spaces in the story.

● TO PLAY

The READER asks each WRITER in turn to call out a word—an adjective or
a noun or whatever the space calls for—and uses them to fill in the blank
spaces in the story. The result is a MAD LIBS® game.

When the READER then reads the completed MAD LIBS® game to the other
players, they will discover that they have written a story that is fantastic,
screamingly funny, shocking, silly, crazy, or just plain dumb—depending
upon which words each WRITER called out.

● EXAMPLE (*Before* and *After*)

" _____ !" he said _____
EXCLAMATION   ADVERB

as he jumped into his convertible _____ and
                                            NOUN

drove off with his _____ wife.
                          ADJECTIVE

" _____OUCH_____ !" he said _____STUPIDLY_____
EXCLAMATION   ADVERB

as he jumped into his convertible _____CAT_____ and
                                            NOUN

drove off with his _____BRAVE_____ wife.
                          ADJECTIVE

In case you have forgotten what adjectives, adverbs, nouns, and verbs are, here is a quick review:

An ADJECTIVE describes something or somebody. *Lumpy*, *soft*, *ugly*, *messy*, and *short* are adjectives.

An ADVERB tells how something is done. It modifies a verb and usually ends in "ly." *Modestly*, *stupidly*, *greedily*, and *carefully* are adverbs.

A NOUN is the name of a person, place, or thing. *Sidewalk*, *umbrella*, *bridle*, *bathtub*, and *nose* are nouns.

A VERB is an action word. *Run*, *pitch*, *jump*, and *swim* are verbs. Put the verbs in past tense if the directions say PAST TENSE. *Ran*, *pitched*, *jumped*, and *swam* are verbs in the past tense.

When we ask for A PLACE, we mean any sort of place: a country or city (*Spain*, *Cleveland*) or a room (*bathroom*, *kitchen*).

An EXCLAMATION or SILLY WORD is any sort of funny sound, gasp, grunt, or outcry, like *Wow!*, *Ouch!*, *Whomp!*, *Ick!*, and *Gadzooks!*

When we ask for specific words, like a NUMBER, a COLOR, an ANIMAL, or a PART OF THE BODY, we mean a word that is one of those things, like *seven*, *blue*, *horse*, or *head*.

When we ask for a PLURAL, it means more than one. For example, *cat* pluralized is *cats*.

MAD LIBS® is fun to play with friends, but you can also play it by yourself! To begin with, DO NOT look at the story on the page below. Fill in the blanks on this page with the words called for. Then, using the words you have selected, fill in the blank spaces in the story.

Now you've created your own hilarious MAD LIBS® game!

STAR-LORD, MAN!

_____ PLURAL NOUN

_____ ADJECTIVE

_____ NOUN

_____ OCCUPATION

_____ ADJECTIVE

_____ VEHICLE

_____ VERB ENDING IN "ING"

_____ ADJECTIVE

_____ OCCUPATION

_____ VERB

_____ VERB

_____ NOUN

_____ ADJECTIVE

_____ PLURAL NOUN

_____ VEHICLE

_____ NOUN

_____ NOUN

MAD LIBS®

STAR-LORD, MAN!

Young Peter Quill was abducted from Earth in 1988 by the

_____, a group of _____ pirates. Now, decades
<u>PLURAL NOUN</u>   <u>ADJECTIVE</u>

after his abduction, Peter feels like he is alone in the _____,
                                                              <u>NOUN</u>

and he spends his time working as a/an _____. Peter's most
                                              <u>OCCUPATION</u>

_____ possessions are his cassette player, a beloved mixtape, and
<u>ADJECTIVE</u>

his _____, the *Milano*. He lives by the code of the
        <u>VEHICLE</u>

Ravagers, _____ from everybody. But when he steals a
            <u>VERB ENDING IN "ING"</u>

very valuable and _____ Orb, a/an _____ is sent to
                      <u>ADJECTIVE</u>   <u>OCCUPATION</u>

_____ him. Still, Peter is determined to _____ the
<u>VERB</u>   <u>VERB</u>

Orb. He forms a/an _____ with a group of _____
                      <u>NOUN</u>   <u>ADJECTIVE</u>

misfits, the _____ of the Galaxy. Traveling in his trusty
                <u>PLURAL NOUN</u>

_____, the *Milano*, he sets out to make a/an _____
<u>VEHICLE</u>   <u>NOUN</u>

for himself: Star-Lord, man! Legendary _____.
                                            <u>NOUN</u>

MAD LIBS® is fun to play with friends, but you can also play it by yourself! To begin with, DO NOT look at the story on the page below. Fill in the blanks on this page with the words called for. Then, using the words you have selected, fill in the blank spaces in the story.

Now you've created your own hilarious MAD LIBS® game!

THE LURE OF THE ORB

ADJECTIVE _____

NOUN _____

ANIMAL _____

ADJECTIVE _____

ADJECTIVE _____

PLURAL NOUN _____

ADVERB _____

PLURAL NOUN _____

ADJECTIVE _____

ADJECTIVE _____

VERB _____

NOUN _____

ADVERB _____

NOUN _____

MAD LIBS

THE LURE OF THE ORB

The stolen Orb is a very _____ artifact. It has a/an
                       ADJECTIVE

_____ of the Covenant or a Maltese _____ kind of
NOUN   ANIMAL

vibe. And although it seems _____, the Orb actually contains
                                 ADJECTIVE

_____ ingots: infinity _____! These stones are
ADJECTIVE   PLURAL NOUN

_____ powerful. They can only be handled by
ADVERB

_____ of very _____ and extraordinary power.
PLURAL NOUN   ADJECTIVE

After Peter Quill tricks Yondu with a/an _____ fake Orb, the
                                       ADJECTIVE

Guardians _____ the real Orb to the Nova Corps. The Orb
               VERB

represents _____. As Tivan the Collector says, "It is such a/an
             NOUN

_____ potent _____."
ADVERB   NOUN

From MARVEL'S GUARDIANS OF THE GALAXY MAD LIBS® • Copyright © 2017 MARVEL.
Published by Mad Libs, an imprint of Penguin Random House LLC.

MAD LIBS® is fun to play with friends, but you can also play it by yourself! To begin with, DO NOT look at the story on the page below. Fill in the blanks on this page with the words called for. Then, using the words you have selected, fill in the blank spaces in the story.

Now you've created your own hilarious MAD LIBS® game!

WELCOME TO XANDAR!

ADJECTIVE _____

VERB _____

NOUN _____

PLURAL NOUN _____

NOUN _____

PLURAL NOUN _____

NOUN _____

ADVERB _____

PLURAL NOUN _____

VERB ENDING IN "ING" _____

VERB (PAST TENSE) _____

ADJECTIVE _____

ADJECTIVE _____

PLURAL NOUN _____

ADJECTIVE _____

MAD LIBS®
WELCOME TO XANDAR!

While in the capital of the _____ Empire, be sure you don't

ADJECTIVE

_____ in the water, you _____! Watch out for

VERB   **NOUN**

bounty hunters and _____, or you may end up in the Kyln

PLURAL NOUN

_____. If you hear these _____, it's too late:

NOUN   **PLURAL NOUN**

"By the _____ of the Nova Corps, you are _____

NOUN   **ADVERB**

under arrest!" Once you are imprisoned in the Kyln, your

_____, along with any orbs you're _____, will

PLURAL NOUN   **VERB ENDING IN "ING"**

be impounded. You'll be _____ with _____

         VERB (PAST TENSE)   **ADJECTIVE**

foam and given a/an _____ jumpsuit. Sleeping is strictly in

         ADJECTIVE

_____ on the floor. Sound _____? Good! Enjoy

PLURAL NOUN   **ADJECTIVE**

your stay!

MAD LIBS® is fun to play with friends, but you can also play it by yourself! To begin with, DO NOT look at the story on the page below. Fill in the blanks on this page with the words called for. Then, using the words you have selected, fill in the blank spaces in the story.

Now you've created your own hilarious MAD LIBS® game!

CHECK OUT THE NEW MEAT

ADJECTIVE _____

NOUN _____

PLURAL NOUN _____

PART OF THE BODY (PLURAL) _____

NOUN _____

VERB (PAST TENSE) _____

PLURAL NOUN _____

NOUN _____

VERB _____

ADJECTIVE _____

ADJECTIVE _____

ADVERB _____

NOUN _____

VERB _____

ADVERB _____

ADJECTIVE _____

ADJECTIVE _____

MAD LIBS®

CHECK OUT THE NEW MEAT

One of the more _____ inmates in the Kyln is Drax, the
                        ADJECTIVE

Destroyer. He's the _____ with the red _____ all
                         NOUN   PLURAL NOUN

over his _____. The first _____ you should
          PART OF THE BODY (PLURAL)   NOUN

know about him is that he's pretty mad! After Ronan

_____ his wife and daughter, Drax slayed dozens of
   VERB (PAST TENSE)

his _____ for revenge. He is a/an _____ on a
        PLURAL NOUN   NOUN

mission! Drax wants to _____ Gamora in revenge, but Peter
                            VERB

Quill convinces him that keeping her alive is a/an _____ idea
                                                        ADJECTIVE

because she can bring Ronan to him. But it is not a/an _____
                                                           ADJECTIVE

idea to make jokes around Drax. His people are _____ literal,
                                                     ADVERB

so Drax has no sense of _____ or irony. Don't *ever*
                             NOUN

_____ him a thesaurus! Because he is _____ strong
     VERB   ADVERB

and super angry, you won't want to mess with this _____
                                                       ADJECTIVE

beast. And if you're _____, you'll work on getting him to join
                          ADJECTIVE

your side!

From MARVEL'S GUARDIANS OF THE GALAXY MAD LIBS® • Copyright © 2017 MARVEL.
Published by Mad Libs, an imprint of Penguin Random House LLC.

MAD LIBS® is fun to play with friends, but you can also play it by yourself! To begin with, DO NOT look at the story on the page below. Fill in the blanks on this page with the words called for. Then, using the words you have selected, fill in the blank spaces in the story.

Now you've created your own hilarious MAD LIBS® game!

THANOS FAMILY TREE

ADJECTIVE ——————————————

ADVERB ——————————————

VERB (PAST TENSE) ——————————————

ADJECTIVE ——————————————

ADJECTIVE ——————————————

PLURAL NOUN ——————————————

ADJECTIVE ——————————————

PART OF THE BODY ——————————————

ADJECTIVE ——————————————

FIRST NAME (FEMALE) ——————————————

VERB ——————————————

NOUN ——————————————

NOUN ——————————————

ADJECTIVE ——————————————

VERB (PAST TENSE) ——————————————

NOUN ——————————————

ADJECTIVE ——————————————

MAD LIBS®

THANOS FAMILY TREE

Nebula and Gamora are the daughters of the _____ Titan,
ADJECTIVE

Thanos. Gamora is _____ his favorite daughter. She is
ADVERB

surgically _____ and trained as a/an _____
VERB (PAST TENSE) _ADJECTIVE_

weapon. Gamora's _____ green skin and excellent fighting
ADJECTIVE

_____ make her a/an _____ standout in this
PLURAL NOUN _ADJECTIVE_

family! On the other _____, Gamora's sister Nebula is totally
PART OF THE BODY

_____. She is jealous of _____, and decides to
ADJECTIVE _FIRST NAME (FEMALE)_

_____ with Ronan against her own _____. But the
VERB _NOUN_

_____ backfires when the sisters meet in _____
NOUN _ADJECTIVE_

battle. Nebula is _____ when the *Dark* _____
VERB (PAST TENSE) _NOUN_

warship is destroyed over Xandar. So much for a/an _____
ADJECTIVE

sisterly bond!

MAD LIBS® is fun to play with friends, but you can also play it by yourself! To begin with, DO NOT look at the story on the page below. Fill in the blanks on this page with the words called for. Then, using the words you have selected, fill in the blank spaces in the story.

Now you've created your own hilarious MAD LIBS® game!

IT'S COOL TO HAVE A CODE NAME

PLURAL NOUN _____

VERB ENDING IN "ING" _____

ADJECTIVE _____

NUMBER _____

NOUN _____

PLURAL NOUN _____

PART OF THE BODY (PLURAL) _____

CELEBRITY (MALE) _____

ADJECTIVE _____

NOUN _____

ADJECTIVE _____

NOUN _____

ADJECTIVE _____

VERB _____

PLURAL NOUN _____

MAD LIBS®
IT'S COOL TO HAVE
A CODE NAME

Some _____ have nicknames and some don't. But if you're

PLURAL NOUN

_____ through the galaxy, it's cool to have a/an

VERB ENDING IN "ING"

_____ name or _____. And outlaw names are even

ADJECTIVE   NUMBER

better!

- Peter Quill's nickname is _____-Lord. On his home

  NOUN

  planet there's a legend about people who have _____

  PLURAL NOUN

  up their _____. A great hero called

  PART OF THE BODY (PLURAL)

  _____ teaches an entire city that dancing is the

  CELEBRITY (MALE)

  most _____ thing there is.

  ADJECTIVE

- Just don't call Rocket a raccoon! Because there "ain't no

  _____ like me, except me!"

  NOUN

- And Groot is known as Rocket's _____ houseplant

  ADJECTIVE

  and _____. Even though Drax calls him a/an

  NOUN

  _____ tree, he won't let anyone else _____ his

  ADJECTIVE   VERB

  friends like that. So what if he has to take _____

  PLURAL NOUN

  from a hamster? The Guardians are all in this together!

MAD LIBS® is fun to play with friends, but you can also play it by yourself! To begin with, DO NOT look at the story on the page below. Fill in the blanks on this page with the words called for. Then, using the words you have selected, fill in the blank spaces in the story.

Now you've created your own hilarious MAD LIBS® game!

THE ROUTE OF THE MILANO

ADJECTIVE _____

VERB _____

ADJECTIVE _____

NOUN _____

VERB _____

ADJECTIVE _____

VERB _____

VERB _____

NOUN _____

ADJECTIVE _____

VERB _____

PLURAL NOUN _____

NOUN _____

ADJECTIVE _____

NOUN _____

VERB ENDING IN "ING" _____

VERB (PAST TENSE) _____

THE ROUTE OF THE *MILANO*

We first see the *Milano*, Peter Quill's _____ spaceship, as he

ADJECTIVE

lands on Morag to _____ the Orb. After Quill makes a/an

VERB

_____ and daring escape, he finds a lovely _____ still

ADJECTIVE _NOUN_

aboard: Bereet. While Quill is on Xandar to _____ the Broker,

VERB

his ship is impounded. But the _____ Guardians are able to

ADJECTIVE

_____ together and retrieve the *Milano*. They _____

VERB _VERB_

to Knowhere to sell the _____ to the Collector—where they

NOUN

run into even more _____ trouble! Rocket, Groot, and Drax

ADJECTIVE

must _____ the Ravagers to save their _____.

VERB _PLURAL NOUN_

The *Milano* later joins with the Ravagers in formation against Ronan's

_____, the *Dark Aster*. After the _____ *Aster* crashes

NOUN _ADJECTIVE_

into their capital _____, the Nova Corps rebuild the *Milano*

NOUN

out of gratitude for _____ Xandar. The newly

VERB ENDING IN "ING"

_____ Guardians of the Galaxy then depart in the

VERB (PAST TENSE)

Milano for their next adventure. Wonder where they're headed now?

MAD LIBS® is fun to play with friends, but you can also play it by yourself! To begin with, DO NOT look at the story on the page below. Fill in the blanks on this page with the words called for. Then, using the words you have selected, fill in the blank spaces in the story.

Now you've created your own hilarious MAD LIBS® game!

"I WAS JUST KIDDING ABOUT THE LEG!"

ADJECTIVE _____

ADJECTIVE _____

PART OF THE BODY _____

ADJECTIVE _____

PART OF THE BODY _____

COLOR _____

ADJECTIVE _____

ADJECTIVE _____

VERB _____

A PLACE _____

VERB ENDING IN "ING" _____

ADJECTIVE _____

MAD☺LIBS®
"I WAS JUST KIDDING ABOUT THE LEG!"

Rocket has a totally _____ plan to escape the Kyln, but first
                      ADJECTIVE

he's going to need a few _____ things:
                         ADJECTIVE

- A security _____ band from one of the guards
             PART OF THE BODY

- A/An _____ _____ from one of the prisoners
       ADJECTIVE PART OF THE BODY

- And a battery from the _____ panel with the
                         COLOR

  _____ yellow light
  ADJECTIVE

Once the _____ gravity is turned off, it's _____ time!
         ADJECTIVE   VERB

Just make sure you remember to recover the Orb from (the)

_____, get the *Milano* up and _____, and of
A PLACE   VERB ENDING IN "ING"

course, find Quill's _____ cassette player. He's got his
                     ADJECTIVE

priorities, after all!

From MARVEL'S GUARDIANS OF THE GALAXY MAD LIBS® • Copyright © 2017 MARVEL.
Published by Mad Libs, an imprint of Penguin Random House LLC.

MAD LIBS® is fun to play with friends, but you can also play it by yourself! To begin with, DO NOT look at the story on the page below. Fill in the blanks on this page with the words called for. Then, using the words you have selected, fill in the blank spaces in the story.

Now you've created your own hilarious MAD LIBS® game!

BLUE MAN

_____ VERB (PAST TENSE)

_____ VERB

_____ NOUN

_____ ADVERB

_____ VERB (PAST TENSE)

_____ VEHICLE

_____ NUMBER

_____ NOUN

_____ ADJECTIVE

_____ NOUN

_____ ADJECTIVE

_____ PLURAL NOUN

_____ ADJECTIVE

_____ PART OF THE BODY

_____ ADJECTIVE

_____ ADJECTIVE

MAD LIBS®

BLUE MAN

Even though Yondu has always _____ Peter Quill, he
                          VERB (PAST TENSE)

swears he's going to _____ him when he finds him. That's
                     VERB

because Yondu wants the _____ that Quill stole. On top of
                        NOUN

that, Yondu _____ expects Quill to be grateful that he hasn't
            ADVERB

_____ him yet! After all, it was Yondu who picked
VERB (PAST TENSE)

Peter up in his _____ on Terra _____ years ago.
                VEHICLE   NUMBER

Yondu is the _____ of the Ravagers. He carries a/an
             NOUN

_____ arrow on his _____ that he controls by
ADJECTIVE   NOUN

whistling. The arrow is sharp and _____. It can tear through
                                  ADJECTIVE

many _____ in one _____ shot. So you better
     PLURAL NOUN   ADJECTIVE

watch your _____, Quill: Yondu is a/an _____
           PART OF THE BODY   ADJECTIVE

negotiator, but he is also a/an _____ pirate!
                                ADJECTIVE

MAD LIBS® is fun to play with friends, but you can also play it by yourself! To begin with, DO NOT look at the story on the page below. Fill in the blanks on this page with the words called for. Then, using the words you have selected, fill in the blank spaces in the story.

Now you've created your own hilarious MAD LIBS® game!

KNOWHERE IN THE GALAXY

_____ ADJECTIVE

_____ NOUN

_____ ADJECTIVE

_____ NOUN

_____ OCCUPATION (PLURAL)

_____ ADJECTIVE

_____ NOUN

_____ PLURAL NOUN

_____ TYPE OF LIQUID

_____ PLURAL NOUN

_____ ADJECTIVE

_____ COLOR

_____ NOUN

_____ VERB ENDING IN "ING"

_____ PLURAL NOUN

_____ EXCLAMATION

_____ NUMBER

MAD LIBS®

KNOWHERE IN THE GALAXY

Last night I had a very _____ dream. I was on an outpost in

ADJECTIVE

outer _____. And that post was deep inside the head of a/an

NOUN

_____ ancient being! I am not kidding! The _____

ADJECTIVE   NOUN

was called "Knowhere" and it was filled with _____ that

OCCUPATION (PLURAL)

were sent by the Tivan Group to mine the _____ matter

ADJECTIVE

within the skull of the _____: bone, brain _____,

NOUN   PLURAL NOUN

and spinal _____. All of these _____ are

TYPE OF LIQUID   PLURAL NOUN

extremely _____ on the _____ market. There was

ADJECTIVE   COLOR

even a/an _____ inside the cantina that had reptiles

NOUN

_____! And the only rule seemed to be that there were

VERB ENDING IN "ING"

"No _____ whatsoever here." _____! Sure

PLURAL NOUN   EXCLAMATION

sounds like a place you wouldn't want to visit for more than _____

NUMBER

days . . . or hours!

From MARVEL'S GUARDIANS OF THE GALAXY MAD LIBS® • Copyright © 2017 MARVEL.
Published by Mad Libs, an imprint of Penguin Random House LLC.

MAD LIBS® is fun to play with friends, but you can also play it by yourself! To begin with, DO NOT look at the story on the page below. Fill in the blanks on this page with the words called for. Then, using the words you have selected, fill in the blank spaces in the story.

Now you've created your own hilarious MAD LIBS® game!

HE'S NOT MY REAL FATHER!

NOUN _____

ADJECTIVE _____

ADJECTIVE _____

NOUN _____

VERB _____

VERB (PAST TENSE) _____

ADJECTIVE _____

VERB _____

PLURAL NOUN _____

NOUN _____

ADJECTIVE _____

NOUN _____

VERB _____

MAD LIBS

HE'S NOT MY REAL FATHER!

Although Gamora is the adopted _____ of Thanos, she is
                                    NOUN

anything but daddy's _____ little girl! Thanos killed Gamora's
                        ADJECTIVE

real family and tortured her. Then he turned her into a/an

_____, green, fighting machine. She is actually an orphan
   ADJECTIVE

and a/an _____. When Quill explains that his job is to
            NOUN

negotiate, while hers is to "Stab! _____! Stab!" Gamora
                                     VERB

reminds him that Thanos never _____ diplomacy. She
                                VERB (PAST TENSE)

gets her chance to get away from the _____ Thanos, but then
                                        ADJECTIVE

Gamora fears she will _____ surrounded by the biggest
                          VERB

_____ in the galaxy! After all, she is a/an _____
   PLURAL NOUN   NOUN

who doesn't dance. She's definitely not some _____-eyed
                                                ADJECTIVE

_____! But eventually Gamora does _____. *And* she
   NOUN   VERB

becomes a Guardian!

MAD LIBS® is fun to play with friends, but you can also play it by yourself! To begin with, DO NOT look at the story on the page below. Fill in the blanks on this page with the words called for. Then, using the words you have selected, fill in the blank spaces in the story.

Now you've created your own hilarious MAD LIBS® game!

TANELEER TIVAN'S COLLECTION

_____ PLURAL NOUN

_____ NOUN

_____ ADJECTIVE

_____ ADJECTIVE

_____ NOUN

_____ FIRST NAME (FEMALE)

_____ ADJECTIVE

_____ ANIMAL

_____ ADJECTIVE

_____ A PLACE

_____ ADJECTIVE

_____ COLOR

_____ ADJECTIVE

_____ NOUN

_____ NOUN

_____ VERB

MAD LIBS®
TANELEER TIVAN'S
COLLECTION

Welcome to the museum! Here you will find _____, relics,
_____ PLURAL NOUN

and specimens of all manner! The museum is Tivan's _____.
_____ NOUN

He runs this _____ place with Karina, his _____,
ADJECTIVE _____ ADJECTIVE

unhinged assistant. Here is a/an _____ containing his previous
_____ NOUN

assistant, _____. She is a/an _____ display here
FIRST NAME (FEMALE) _____ ADJECTIVE

among the frogs, ducks, and other _____ oddities.
_____ ANIMAL

Tivan even has a/an _____ dog, ready for his mission to
_____ ADJECTIVE

(the) _____! Don't let Tivan's _____ glasses
A PLACE _____ ADJECTIVE

and _____ nail polish alarm you. He is a/an _____
COLOR _____ ADJECTIVE

collector! He's even interested in the _____, Groot. But he'll
_____ NOUN

politely wait until the _____ of his death to add him to the
NOUN

collection. His real wish, of course, is to _____ the Orb!
_____ VERB

From MARVEL'S GUARDIANS OF THE GALAXY MAD LIBS® • Copyright © 2017 MARVEL.
Published by Mad Libs, an imprint of Penguin Random House LLC.

MAD LIBS® is fun to play with friends, but you can also play it by yourself. To begin with, DO NOT look at the story on the page below. Fill in the blanks on this page with the words called for. Then, using the words you have selected, fill in the blank spaces in the story.

Now you've created your own hilarious MAD LIBS® game!

WHAT HAS THE GALAXY EVER DONE FOR YOU?

_____ PLURAL NOUN

_____ NUMBER

_____ VERB

_____ NOUN

_____ VERB

_____ PLURAL NOUN

_____ VERB

_____ PLURAL NOUN

_____ ADJECTIVE

_____ NOUN

_____ PLURAL NOUN

_____ VERB

_____ ADJECTIVE

_____ VERB

_____ PLURAL NOUN

MAD LIBS®
WHAT HAS THE GALAXY
EVER DONE FOR YOU?

Quill: This is why none of you have any _____!
                                              PLURAL NOUN

_____ seconds after you meet someone, you're ready to
NUMBER

_____ 'em!
VERB

Rocket: What are you, a/an _____? Why would you want to
                                    NOUN

_____ the universe? What's it ever done for you?
VERB

Quill: Well, I'm one of the _____ who live here! I
                                      PLURAL NOUN

_____ around, and you know what I see? Losers! I mean . . .
VERB

_____ who have lost stuff!
PLURAL NOUN

Drax: You're _____. I was a/an _____. All the anger,
                    ADJECTIVE   NOUN

all the _____. It was just to _____ my loss.
            PLURAL NOUN   VERB

Gamora: Everybody's lost _____ people. It's no excuse to
                                  ADJECTIVE

_____ everyone else dead.
VERB

Rocket: You're making me . . . beat up . . . _____!
                                                      PLURAL NOUN

MAD LIBS® is fun to play with friends, but you can also play it by yourself! To begin with, DO NOT look at the story on the page below. Fill in the blanks on this page with the words called for. Then, using the words you have selected, fill in the blank spaces in the story.

Now you've created your own hilarious MAD LIBS® game!

LOST IN SPACE

_____ ADJECTIVE

_____ PLURAL NOUN

_____ VERB

_____ VEHICLE

_____ ADVERB

_____ NOUN

_____ ADJECTIVE

_____ VERB

_____ VERB

_____ ADJECTIVE

_____ COLOR

_____ ARTICLE OF CLOTHING

_____ ADJECTIVE

_____ VERB

_____ PLURAL NOUN

_____ ADJECTIVE

_____ ADJECTIVE

MAD LIBS®

LOST IN SPACE

Here are some _____ survival tips if you find yourself or your
_____ADJECTIVE_____

_____ floating in space:
___PLURAL NOUN___

- Pods aren't meant to _____ in space, so get to the
  _____VERB_____

  _____ as _____ as you can!
  ___VEHICLE___   ___ADVERB___

- Remember: The _____ is in the _____ pod—
  _____NOUN_____ADJECTIVE_____

  _____ there first!
  ___VERB___

- Don't _____ the Orb!
  ___VERB___

- Use your long _____ branch arm to pull your big
  _____ADJECTIVE_____

  _____ friend out of the goo!
  _____COLOR_____

- If you can fire your rocket _____, you'll be
  _____ARTICLE OF CLOTHING_____

  fine.

- Always give your _____ mask to a friend. She will
  _____ADJECTIVE_____

  _____ you for it later.
  ___VERB___

- If your _____ have to rescue you, that's a/an
  ___PLURAL NOUN___

  _____ thing.
  ___ADJECTIVE___

- Sometimes it's better to be _____ than dead!
  _____ADJECTIVE_____

From MARVEL'S GUARDIANS OF THE GALAXY MAD LIBS® • Copyright © 2017 MARVEL.
Published by Mad Libs, an imprint of Penguin Random House LLC.

MAD LIBS® is fun to play with friends, but you can also play it by yourself. To begin with, DO NOT look at the story on the page below. Fill in the blanks on this page with the words called for. Then, using the words you have selected, fill in the blank spaces in the story.

Now you've created your own hilarious MAD LIBS® game!

I AM GROOT

NOUN _____

ADJECTIVE _____

ANIMAL _____

ADJECTIVE _____

PLURAL NOUN _____

NOUN _____

VEHICLE _____

ADJECTIVE _____

EXCLAMATION _____

PLURAL NOUN _____

VERB (PAST TENSE) _____

ADJECTIVE _____

VERB ENDING IN "ING" _____

MAD LIBS

I AM GROOT

Groot, the humanoid _____, has a very _____
                            NOUN   ADJECTIVE

vocabulary! He's best friends with a/an _____ named Rocket.
                                           ANIMAL

Rocket might accuse Groot of being asleep for the danger, and

awake for all the _____ stuff, but they're still best
                        ADJECTIVE

_____ until the end. In fact, Rocket is the only
        PLURAL NOUN

_____ who understands what Groot says. After Rocket
     NOUN

rescues Groot and Drax in the _____, he interprets the
                                     VEHICLE

_____ tree's thoughts: "_____?! How?! I
   ADJECTIVE   EXCLAMATION

know they're the only _____ we _____!"
                         PLURAL NOUN   VERB (PAST TENSE)

It sure takes a/an _____ friend to understand a walking,
                       ADJECTIVE

_____ tree, but Rocket does!
   VERB ENDING IN "ING"

From MARVEL'S GUARDIANS OF THE GALAXY MAD LIBS® • Copyright © 2017 MARVEL.
Published by Mad Libs, an imprint of Penguin Random House LLC.

MAD LIBS® is fun to play with friends, but you can also play it by yourself! To begin with, DO NOT look at the story on the page below. Fill in the blanks on this page with the words called for. Then, using the words you have selected, fill in the blank spaces in the story.

Now you've created your own hilarious MAD LIBS® game!

ROCKET: NO ONE QUITE LIKE HIM

ADVERB _____

ANIMAL _____

ADJECTIVE _____

PLURAL NOUN _____

ADJECTIVE _____

ADJECTIVE _____

ADJECTIVE _____

VERB _____

PLURAL NOUN _____

PART OF THE BODY _____

VERB _____

NUMBER _____

PART OF THE BODY (PLURAL) _____

MAD LIBS®
ROCKET: NO ONE QUITE LIKE HIM

Specs:

- A/An _____ engineered _____ who functions
  ADVERB   ANIMAL

  as a/an _____ hunter and mercenary.
            ADJECTIVE

- Master of _____, weapons, and _____
              PLURAL NOUN   ADJECTIVE

  tactics.

- A/An _____ fighting machine.
        ADJECTIVE

- An illegal genetic experiment on a/an _____ life form.
                                          ADJECTIVE

Habits:

- Has been known to _____ up _____.
                       VERB   PLURAL NOUN

- Didn't ask to get made!

- Has a/an _____ of gold.
            PART OF THE BODY

- Does not _____ what a raccoon is.
             VERB

Warnings:

- Has escaped _____ prisons.
                NUMBER

- Loves fake _____!
               PART OF THE BODY (PLURAL)

From MARVEL'S GUARDIANS OF THE GALAXY MAD LIBS® • Copyright © 2017 MARVEL.
Published by Mad Libs, an imprint of Penguin Random House LLC.

MAD LIBS® is fun to play with friends, but you can also play it by yourself! To begin with, DO NOT look at the story on the page below. Fill in the blanks on this page with the words called for. Then, using the words you have selected, fill in the blank spaces in the story.

Now you've created your own hilarious MAD LIBS® game!

GO! GO! GUARDIANS!

VEHICLE _____

NOUN _____

ADJECTIVE _____

NOUN _____

FIRST NAME (MALE) _____

PLURAL NOUN _____

ADJECTIVE _____

ADJECTIVE _____

NOUN _____

PLURAL NOUN _____

ADJECTIVE _____

PLURAL NOUN _____

MAD LIBS

GO! GO! GUARDIANS!

After Rocket, Drax, and Groot escape the Ravagers' _____,
                                                        VEHICLE

they all agree that they need a/an _____ to stop Ronan. Quill
                                        NOUN

has a/an _____ idea and tells the group: "Life has given us
              ADJECTIVE

a/an _____. I'm not going to stand by and let _____
         NOUN   FIRST NAME (MALE)

wipe out millions of _____." The Guardians will have to
                          PLURAL NOUN

take some _____ chances, but they are up for the
                ADJECTIVE

_____ challenge. Then, Gamora tells the group: "I have lived
  ADJECTIVE

most of my _____ surrounded by my _____.
                NOUN   PLURAL NOUN

I would be _____ to die among my _____."
                ADJECTIVE   PLURAL NOUN

MAD LIBS® is fun to play with friends, but you can also play it by yourself! To begin with, DO NOT look at the story on the page below. Fill in the blanks on this page with the words called for. Then, using the words you have selected, fill in the blank spaces in the story.

Now you've created your own hilarious MAD LIBS® game!

THE HEALING POWER OF PLANTS

_____ NOUN

_____ ADVERB

_____ ADJECTIVE

_____ VERB

_____ PLURAL NOUN

_____ VERB

_____ ADJECTIVE

_____ VERB

_____ NOUN

_____ VERB

_____ ADJECTIVE

_____ PLURAL NOUN

_____ ADJECTIVE

_____ ADJECTIVE

_____ ADJECTIVE

MAD LIBS®
THE HEALING POWER OF PLANTS

The _____-like humanoid called Groot is _____
      NOUN   ADVERB

deadly, yet sweet. He has many _____ powers. Because he is
                                      ADJECTIVE

part plant, Groot can _____ at will. He is capable of sprouting
                              VERB

_____ whenever he feels like it. His branches make spores
 PLURAL NOUN

that _____ and illuminate _____ spaces. Groot can
        VERB   ADJECTIVE

even _____ many enemies at once. But his most amazing
        VERB

_____ is the ability to _____ a/an _____
    NOUN   VERB   ADJECTIVE

nest to save his _____. Groot makes the _____
              PLURAL NOUN   ADJECTIVE

sacrifice to protect the Guardians, demonstrating the _____
                                          ADJECTIVE

power of plants. Some say he's the real _____ hero of the
                              ADJECTIVE

Guardians!

HOW TO DISTRACT YOUR ENEMY WITH A DANCE-OFF

ADJECTIVE ————————————

VERB ————————————

ADVERB ————————————

NOUN ————————————

PLURAL NOUN ————————————

VERB ————————————

ADJECTIVE ————————————

NOUN ————————————

PLURAL NOUN ————————————

ADJECTIVE ————————————

ADJECTIVE ————————————

PART OF THE BODY (PLURAL) ————————————

NOUN ————————————

VERB ENDING IN "ING" ————————————

ADJECTIVE ————————————

SILLY WORD ————————————

MAD LIBS® is fun to play with friends, but you can also play it by yourself! To begin with, DO NOT look at the story on the page below. Fill in the blanks on this page with the words called for. Then, using the words you have selected, fill in the blank spaces in the story.

Now you've created your own hilarious MAD LIBS® game!

MAD⊚LIBS®
HOW TO DISTRACT YOUR ENEMY WITH A DANCE-OFF

The rules of a dance-off are simple:

1. Choose the _____ song.
   ADJECTIVE

2. Really _____ to the lyrics.
   VERB

3. Bring it _____ hard!
   ADVERB

4. _____-off, Bro!
   NOUN

5. Keep your _____ subtle, then _____ it
   PLURAL NOUN   VERB

   back.

6. Show 'em your _____ moves!
   ADJECTIVE

7. Distract your _____ while your _____
   NOUN   PLURAL NOUN

   shoot the _____ hammer and release the _____
   ADJECTIVE   ADJECTIVE

   stone!

8. Everybody hold _____.
   PART OF THE BODY (PLURAL)

9. State your _____ clearly while _____.
   NOUN   VERB ENDING IN "ING"

10. This would be a/an _____ time to call your opponent
    ADJECTIVE

    a/an _____ .
    SILLY WORD

11. Claim victory!

MAD LIBS® is fun to play with friends, but you can also play it by yourself! To begin with, DO NOT look at the story on the page below. Fill in the blanks on this page with the words called for. Then, using the words you have selected, fill in the blank spaces in the story.

Now you've created your own hilarious MAD LIBS® game!

WE ARE GROOT

ADJECTIVE _____

ADJECTIVE _____

ADJECTIVE _____

ADJECTIVE _____

PLURAL NOUN _____

ADJECTIVE _____

NOUN _____

NOUN _____

NOUN _____

NOUN _____

PLURAL NOUN _____

ADVERB _____

VEHICLE _____

MAD LIBS

WE ARE GROOT

Dear Advice Lady,

My _____ ship has been destroyed! Will I ever feel
     ADJECTIVE

_____ again?
   ADJECTIVE

Peter Quill, a.k.a. Star-Lord

Dear Peter,

Yes! You've learned many _____ lessons along the way, so
                              ADJECTIVE

remember to be grateful for the _____ things in life, like
                                    ADJECTIVE

_____ to sit among the rubble with, a/an _____
   PLURAL NOUN   ADJECTIVE

orb to trick your enemies, or a small _____ of dirt to keep
                                            NOUN

your _____ in. Your criminal _____ has been
        NOUN   NOUN

expunged and your father is an ancient _____! Your
                                            NOUN

_____ are your family now. And the Nova Corps are
   PLURAL NOUN

_____ grateful.
   ADVERB

I think you'll find a new _____ very soon!
                              VEHICLE

Sincerely,

Advice Lady

From MARVEL'S GUARDIANS OF THE GALAXY MAD LIBS® • Copyright © 2017 MARVEL.
Published by Mad Libs, an imprint of Penguin Random House LLC.

MAD LIBS® is fun to play with friends, but you can also play it by yourself. To begin with, DO NOT look at the story on the page below. Fill in the blanks on this page with the words called for. Then, using the words you have selected, fill in the blank spaces in the story.

Now you've created your own hilarious MAD LIBS® game!

MIXTAPE VOL. 1

NOUN _____

ADJECTIVE _____

ADJECTIVE _____

ADJECTIVE _____

PLURAL NOUN _____

ADJECTIVE _____

ADJECTIVE _____

NOUN _____

ADVERB _____

ADJECTIVE _____

ADJECTIVE _____

NOUN _____

FIRST NAME _____

MAD LIBS

MIXTAPE VOL. 1

So, you want to make a mixtape just like Quill's? Just follow these tried-and-true guidelines!

- Find a cassette _____ and a/an _____ tape.
  NOUN   ADJECTIVE

  Garage sales are one _____ place to start.
  ADJECTIVE

- Think of your favorite songs about friendship or the most

  _____ love _____ you know.
  ADJECTIVE   PLURAL NOUN

- Music that evokes _____ memories of _____
  ADJECTIVE   ADJECTIVE

  childhood adventures—or a family _____—is
  NOUN

  _____ a good idea.
  ADVERB

- It's always a/an _____ idea to include a/an _____
  ADJECTIVE   ADJECTIVE

  note along with your mixtape. Maybe something like: "You

  are my little _____. Love, _____."
  NOUN   FIRST NAME